P9-DNS-841

SECRET OF THE STAIRCASE

By Steven K. Smith

MyBoys3 Press

Copyright © 2015 by Steven K. Smith

MyBoys3 Press

Editing by: Kim Sheard (anotherviewediting.com)

Book Cover Design by www.ebooklaunch.com

This is a work of fiction. Names, characters, places and incidents either are the product of of the author's imagination or are used fictitiously. Any resemblance to actual persons, living or dead, events or locales is entirely coincidental.

All rights reserved. No part of this book may be reproduced in any form or by any electronic or mechanical means, including information storage and retrieval systems, without written permission from the author, except for the use of brief quotations in a book review.

For more information, contact us at:

MyBoys3 Press, P.O. Box 2555, Midlothian, VA 23113

www.myboys3.com

Third Printing

ISBN: 978-0-9893414-5-5

To Haley and Drew

SECRET
OF THE
STAIRCASE

CHAPTER ONE

S am tugged on the top button of his collared shirt. It was too tight. He wondered if it was possible to die from shirt collar strangulation. He'd never heard of anyone dying that way, but right then it seemed possible.

He hated wasting a perfectly good Saturday shopping for dress clothes with his mom and brother, Derek. This wasn't much better than fifth grade math class.

His mom draped three brightly colored ties over the dressing room door. "See which one of these you like best."

"Mom..." Sam groaned. "Why do I need to wear a suit anyway?"

"It's going to be an elegant wedding," answered his mom. "I need you to look nice for the pictures. Anita deserves to have special memories of her big day. I haven't seen her since she moved overseas. That's where she met Robert, in England."

1

"But I'm not even *in* the wedding. Why would anyone be taking pictures of me?" Anita was Mom's college roommate. She was getting married in a week, and Sam and Derek were supposed to hand out programs before the ceremony. Derek had asked if they could charge money for each program, like at a baseball game, but Mom said no.

"Why don't you wear your birthday suit, Sam?" a voice called over the wall from the next dressing room stall. "That would make some really special memories!"

Sam shot a dirty look through the wall as his older brother cracked up at his own joke. "Laugh if you want to, Derek, but you'll be wearing a suit too, you know." He stepped out of the dressing room and held the three ties up in front of him in a big, angled mirror. He could see every side of himself, and each one looked stupid in the suit.

Derek walked out of his dressing room and stood next to Sam. "Yeah," he said, running his fingers through his hair, "but I make a suit look good." He struck a pose as if he were the coolest kid in the entire seventh grade.

Oh brother, thought Sam.

"The Jefferson is a very fancy hotel," said Mom. "You'll be expected to look your best."

Sam perked up at the name. "You mean like Thomas Jefferson? We're staying at his house?" He grinned. That would be cool, suit or no suit.

"No, not Thomas Jefferson's house," said Mom. "That's Monticello, out near Charlottesville. This is The

Jefferson hotel. It was named after Thomas Jefferson, but it's in downtown Richmond."

"Never heard of it," said Derek. "It's fancy?"

Mom nodded. "Very fancy, and very old." She held the yellow tie under Sam's chin and frowned. "And very expensive. That's why you've never been there."

"But now we can go?" asked Derek. "Because of the wedding?"

"That's right," answered Mom. "I like the blue one," she said, decisively. "What do you think, Sam?"

"Sure." It was pointless to argue. It wouldn't make a difference. If it were up to him, he'd wear his basketball high tops and a t-shirt to the wedding. The sooner they got out of this store the better.

"Perfect!" said Mom. "Then I think we're all done. Why don't you boys change back into your other clothes and I'll pay for all this."

"Thank goodness," muttered Sam.

"Unless," continued Mom, "you want to keep shopping..." She raised her eyebrows at them hopefully.

"No!" the boys said quickly. They'd been there too long already. Sometimes it seemed like Mom used events like this to make them try on clothes because she didn't have any daughters to do that with regularly. Both of them rushed back into the cubicles to get undressed.

Mom frowned, but seemed content with what they'd picked out. Her cell phone buzzed, and she quickly retrieved it from her purse.

"Anita!" she exclaimed. "How are you? Have you

landed?" Sam watched her hand grab the clothes he'd laid over the door of the changing room. He could hear her talking all the way to the checkout counter.

"This is going to be a disaster," said Derek, stepping out of the dressing room.

Sam nodded his head. "Tell me about it."

CHAPTER TWO

When they got home, the boys carried their bags from the minivan toward the house. Sam had a hard time keeping his long suit bag from dragging on the ground while also carrying two other bags that held shirts, a tie, a belt, socks and dress shoes. He felt like a pack mule. There had to be enough clothing for five weddings. He'd never been to one before, but he doubted that it could be worth all this.

Sam shivered in the cool breeze. Even though it didn't get as cold in Virginia as it had back in their old home up north, January was still brisk.

Despite the temperature, Sam's dad was standing in the front yard talking to their crusty old neighbor, Mr. Haskins. He was in his eighties and was nice enough, but a little kooky.

"Well, well," said Mr. Haskins. "Where are you boys

off to? Did your folks finally wise up and decide to ship you off to military school?"

Their dad laughed. "We haven't gotten to that point quite yet." He looked over at the boys. "But it could be something to keep in mind." With a nod to Mr. Haskins, he followed their mom into the house. "Talk to you later, Jonas."

"We have a wedding," said Derek, after their dad had gone inside.

"A wedding, eh?" said Mr. Haskins, smiling. "You boys are a little young to be getting hitched, aren't you?" He let out a dry cackle that sounded like a frog.

Sam rolled his eyes. Mr. Haskins was always giving them a hard time. He liked to lecture about how kids these days don't have any manners and play too many video games. Even though he wasn't sure what *getting hitched* meant, he knew it wasn't anything to do with them. "It's our mom's friend."

"It's at The Jefferson," said Derek. "Ever hear of it?"

Mr. Haskins' eyes brightened, and he let out another cackle. "Hear of it? Why, I've heard of it all right." He reached his hands into his pants pockets, pulling out his wallet.

"Are you going to pay us for going to the wedding?" said Derek, nudging Sam in the ribs with his elbow.

"Oh, sure, how much do you want?"

"Really?" said Derek, his eyes brightening.

Mr. Haskins waved his hand in disgust. "Ah, you'd believe anything, boy. Those video games are melting your brain, I'll tell you what." He pulled a square piece of paper out of his wallet and held it in front of Sam. It was an old black-and-white photograph. The edges were crumpled from being in the wallet.

"That's at The Jefferson," said Mr. Haskins. "A long time ago."

Sam glanced down at the picture, then leaned in closer. A tall man in an old-fashioned uniform stood next to a shaggy-haired boy in a fancy room.

Derek crowded in to get a look. "Is that you?"

Mr. Haskins nodded. "I'm the little guy. My pap was the head bellman at The Jefferson for over forty years. When I finished school, I worked there for a spell too."

"No way!" said Derek. "You worked there?"

Mr. Haskins nodded. "Yes siree. Quite a place, that hotel. And all kinds of famous people came through there...presidents, businessmen, celebrities..." He leaned down and looked at them with wide eyes. "Once, I carried the bags of Mr. Elvis Presley."

Sam scrunched his eyebrows. "Who?"

Mr. Haskins placed his hand on his forehead. "You've gotta be kidding me, boy."

"Elvis, Sam," said Derek. "You know..." He twisted his hips in a strange little dance and sang in a goofy voice. "I'm all shook up, uh-huh!"

Sam just stared at him blankly. Maybe his brother had finally lost his mind.

Derek grinned. "You're a little young to understand."

Sam scowled at his brother as Mr. Haskins nodded.

"I kid you not. 1956. He was playing at the Mosque Theatre. I showed him to his room."

"Wow. That's pretty cool," said Derek.

Sam looked closer at the picture. There was something really strange about it. A fountain in the background had something large in the water. He knew what it looked like, but that was impossible.

Sam pointed at the picture. "What's that thing in the fountain? It looks like an alligator."

"Hotels don't have alligators in fountains," said Derek, laughing.

Mr. Haskins chuckled. "This one did. The hotel kept them as pets over the years."

Sam focused on the fountain again. It *was* an alligator! It was stretched out in the water, looking like it could reach up and chomp on the boy at any moment. There didn't seem to be a cage. Who would leave a real alligator loose with people around? That was crazy.

"They were gone when I worked there," said Mr. Haskins, "but a few were still around when I visited my pap as a boy. It was wild!"

"You can say that again!" exclaimed Derek.

Mr. Haskins smiled. "One of my favorite stories about The Jefferson was when an alligator wandered away from the lobby and into the library."

Sam's eyes grew wider. "It did?" His stomach turned. He couldn't imagine staying at a place where alligators roamed free. It was way too dangerous.

Mr. Haskins nodded.

"What did it do in the library?" asked Derek.

"Well," continued Mr. Haskins, "an older woman was sitting in the library reading, and she somehow mistook the alligator for a footstool."

"What?" exclaimed Derek.

"She sat on it?" asked Sam.

"Well, she put her feet on it, at least," said Mr. Haskins. "Suddenly, her footstool started to walk away from her, and she nearly lost it." He chuckled. "Must have been quite the scene, eh?"

Sam nodded his head. "What did she do?"

"Aw, she ran out of the library as fast as she could."

"I don't blame her," said Sam.

"That's crazy," said Derek.

Mr. Haskins grinned. "Like I said, quite a place, that hotel."

Dad stuck his head out the front door. "Boys, lunch is ready."

Sam took a breath, taking in Mr. Haskins' story. "All right, well…see you later." He handed the picture back to his neighbor.

"Yeah, thanks for showing us the picture," said Derek. "We'll tell you if anything like that happens at the wedding."

Mr. Haskins stepped toward his house and waved. "Good luck, boys. And look out for those gators."

CHAPTER THREE

"**B**oys, come on. We're going to be late!" Mom called up the stairs. It was early Friday afternoon and time to leave for The Jefferson. How could one wedding take all weekend? It seemed like such a waste. But Mom said that was part of the deal since it was a super-fancy wedding.

"Most people would be happy to spend a free night in a luxury hotel," she'd said.

"Maybe a free trip to Yankee stadium," Sam had replied, "but not at a wedding."

Mom and Dad had spent the entire morning out doing wedding-related things already. Mom went to a spa with the bride, Anita. They got their nails done or some other girly thing that she was all excited about. Dad played a round of golf at an exclusive country club that he hadn't ever played at before. Anita's fiancé had pulled some strings to get them in.

Mom and Dad swung by to pick the boys up after they were done. The boys begrudgingly piled into the minivan with their suitcases. Sam let out a groan as they pulled out of the driveway. "There's still time to change your mind," he said to his parents.

"Yeah, we could stay home by ourselves," said Derek. "We'd be fine!"

Dad laughed. "Oh sure. That would work out *really* well."

Sam knew his dad was probably right. Over the summer, their cousin Meghan had watched them for a week while his parents went on a trip to Paris. It got a little out of hand. He couldn't imagine his parents making the same mistake twice.

"Anita is one of my dearest friends," said Mom. "I want us to be there to support her at her wedding."

"She's your friend, not ours," said Derek.

Mom ignored their attitudes. "After all these years, she seems to have finally found the right guy."

"I'll say," mumbled Dad, from the front seat. "She hit the jackpot with him."

"Honey!" Mom shot a dirty look at Dad. "She says he's a wonderful man."

"I'm sure he is," said Dad. "But it doesn't hurt that he's loaded."

Sam turned his head. "Loaded? What does that mean?"

Their mom looked back at them. "Anita's fiancé owns

a successful computer software business in England. So he's very well-off."

"You mean, he's rich!" said Derek.

"Yep," nodded Dad.

"Honey..." said Mom, a look of exasperation on her face.

"What? He is," replied Dad. He looked at the boys in the rear-view mirror. "Which is not the most important thing or why Anita is marrying him. But it *is* nice that he's putting the entire wedding party up at The Jefferson."

They exited the expressway and continued onto the narrow side streets of downtown. Mom turned around in her seat. "Dad and I are going to be very busy while we are there. I don't want to have to worry about you two causing trouble." Dad braked at a stop sign. "This is not a basketball court," Mom continued. "It's an elegant hotel. There's not going to be any running around. Understand?"

"No sweat, Mom," said Derek. "You can count on us." He gave Sam a quick wink.

"I saw that, mister," said Mom.

"Saw what?" Derek raised his palms in the air like he was innocent.

Mom just shook her head, and then gave them both a serious look. "There's one more thing I haven't told you yet."

"Oh boy, here it comes," moaned Derek.

Sam didn't know what Mom was going to say, but he

could tell it was going to be bad. "What is it, Mom, do we have to *sing* at the wedding too?"

"Maybe I could sing a solo," said Derek, holding a water bottle up to his mouth like a microphone. "What's a good wedding ballad, Mom?"

"No, I'm not going to make you sing," answered Mom. "But I do need you to be nice to someone."

"Who?" asked Sam.

"Well, Anita's fiancé has a son that's just about your age."

"He does?" said Sam.

"Yes," continued Mom. "His name is Nathan, and you may need to spend some time with him."

"Do you need me to babysit him like I do Sam?" asked Derek, patting Sam on the shoulder like he was two years old.

"Quit it!" Sam swiped the hand away. He was sick of his brother acting like he was ten years older than him rather than just two. Middle school seemed to have made his head even bigger than it normally was.

"Derek, that's enough," said their dad. "Listen to your mother."

"Sorry," said Derek. "So what's the deal with this kid? Is he a loser or something?"

"Derek!"

"Sorry," said Derek again.

"Nathan has apparently been having a tough time accepting that his dad is getting married to Anita and that they'll be moving to the United States," said Mom.

13

"So he's angry?" asked Sam. That seemed understandable. He couldn't imagine either of his parents getting married to someone else, although he heard that it happened a lot. He knew a bunch of kids at school whose parents were divorced. Some even had stepbrothers and -sisters.

"Probably," said Mom, "but I'm sure he's very nice." She turned around again and looked them in the eyes. "Just be kind to him, okay?"

"Got it, Mom," said Derek.

Sam was about to agree, when something caught his attention out the window. "Whoa, is this the hotel?" Sam pushed his face against the window. A light-colored building of tan bricks stood in front of them. It looked like it was four or five stories high. Narrow clock towers rose up on either side of the building, reaching even higher. A round sign stood out front.

The Jefferson Hotel – 1895.

Yep, this was it.

Dad pulled the car forward into a wide, curving driveway. He stopped next to the main entrance. A man dressed in a uniform and a hat eagerly jogged over to them.

"You're parking *here*?" asked Derek.

"I think you'll block the driveway," said Sam. He couldn't see a parking lot. Maybe they should park on the street. This guy was probably going to yell at them.

"Everybody out," said Mom, smiling.

As they all stepped out, Dad handed his keys to the man with the hat. The man gave Dad a slip of paper and hopped into their car.

"Dad! He's taking the van!" shouted Derek.

"He's the valet, it's okay," said Mom, chuckling.

"What's a val-lay?" asked Sam carefully. Maybe it was the name for someone who stole your car. Although Dad did surrender his keys fairly willingly, and neither he nor Mom looked very upset.

Dad handed their luggage to another uniformed man with a cart on wheels and ushered them onto the curb.

"A valet is a parking attendant," said Mom. "It's a service for guests of a nice restaurant or a hotel. That way you don't have to worry about finding a parking spot yourself. They're offering free valet parking to everyone in the wedding party."

"Oh," said Sam, thinking about it. "I guess that's pretty cool."

"How do you know he won't steal your car?" asked Derek.

"That's why I have a receipt," said Dad. He held up the small piece of paper the man gave him. "When we're ready to leave, we'll give this to the valet and he'll run and get our car for us."

How could Dad be so sure? "I think our car is a lot more valuable than that little piece of paper, Dad. I think you should've asked for something else from him."

"Yeah, maybe you should get his wallet," said Derek.

Mom and Dad laughed. "Trust me, boys. It will be fine," said Dad.

Sam watched the man carefully as he drove around the corner in their van. It was a long walk home if the van was stolen. He turned back to the hotel and stepped around a stone column in the entranceway. A dark shape was spread out on the sidewalk in front of him. His heart froze.

It was a giant alligator!

"Whoa!" he shouted. He jumped back into the parking lot, tripping over the luggage cart and landing face-first on Mom's pink suitcase.

Derek laughed. "Smooth, Sam!"

Sam stood up and pointed toward the sidewalk, his heart pounding. "An alligator!"

Derek was still laughing. Sam peered around the column. It was just a statue.

Derek stepped next to him and patted his back gently. "It's okay, buddy. Maybe you should go to the spa with Mom to relax a little."

Sam took a deep breath and stared at the statue. It was probably ten feet long. And even though it was made of bronze, it looked pretty fierce. He read the small sign next to the statue.

"Alligators once lived in marble ponds that surrounded the Thomas Jefferson statue in the Palm Court Lobby. The last of the alligators, Old Pompey, called The Jefferson home until his death in 1948."

Sam looked over at Derek. "Old Pompey, I wonder if that's the one that Mr. Haskins told us about."

"Boys, come on!" called Mom from the entrance door.

Sam followed Derek into the hotel, his eyes peeled for any other lurking reptiles – bronze or otherwise.

CHAPTER FOUR

S am walked into a colorful, light-filled lobby. Tilting his head back, he stared at the huge, round stained glass ceiling. The glass pattern was made up of brilliant blues and reds. "Wow," he whispered.

The light from the ceiling focused onto the middle of the room, where a tall white statue was fenced off from the rest of the space.

"Cool statue," said Derek.

"Do you know who that is?" asked Mom, walking up from the front desk.

"That's easy," said Sam. He'd known even before he saw the inscription along the base. "It's Thomas Jefferson." She should give him a little bit of credit. It *was* the name of the hotel after all.

"Sam! Derek!" called a familiar voice. The boys looked to their left and saw Caitlin running up toward them. "Hey guys, isn't this place great?"

Sam turned to his mom. "What's Caitlin doing here?" He hadn't expected his friend from school to be at the hotel. She wasn't in the wedding. He didn't think she even knew Mom's friend, Anita.

"Didn't I tell you? Caitlin's dad is the photographer for the wedding," said Mom.

"Surprise!" Caitlin smiled and gave him a big hug. Sam turned red and squirmed free of her embrace.

Sam was surprised. But not disappointed. It was fun to have Caitlin along. They'd had cool adventures together in Williamsburg and on Belle Isle. She was super smart, and once he got to know her, she wasn't as annoying as he used to think she was.

Derek nudged Sam in the ribs and bounced his eyebrows with a smirk. He liked to tease that she was Sam's girlfriend, but they were just friends. After all, who needs a girlfriend in fifth grade, anyway?

"Oh, look," said Mom. "There's Anita! Boys, why don't you explore the hotel with Caitlin for a while." She gave them a serious look. "Please talk to Nathan when you see him. And remember what we talked about, this is a nice hotel." She smiled weakly at Caitlin. "Make sure they don't get crazy."

"Yes, ma'am. I'll do my best," said Caitlin.

"Let's go," said Derek, leading them to the edge of the lobby. "I want to look for more alligators."

Derek stopped at a balcony that looked out over an enormous open room. As much as Sam had been impressed with the stained glass ceiling and the statue in the upstairs entrance, he had to stop and marvel at this bigger room.

"Isn't it beautiful?" said Caitlin.

Sam felt like he had walked into a palace. The Rotunda was over two stories high with a balcony wrapping all around. Ornate marble columns were built into the walls, stacked above and below the balcony from floor to ceiling. Potted palm trees filled each corner of the room. Several fine-leather couches and dark-wood tables were scattered on an elegant carpet in the center of the white marble floor. The ceiling stretched above them, decorated in the middle with more stained glass and fancy designs. Sam made a quick scan for alligators, but didn't see any.

"Look at the staircase," said Caitlin, walking to the center of the balcony. A long, elaborate staircase descended down into the Rotunda. It was wider than a normal staircase. An elegant red carpet stretched across the steps. They walked down two sets of five steps and stopped to gaze down the final set of a couple dozen.

"That's impressive," said Derek, approaching from behind them with a whistle. "It looks like something. I just can't think of what."

"A staircase?" asked Sam.

Caitlin giggled. "People think it looks just like the staircase in 'Gone With the Wind.' That's one of my mom's favorite movies. Have you seen it?"

Sam shook his head. It sounded familiar, though.

"It's a love story set on a southern plantation during

the Civil War. It's a classic."

The Civil War part sounded okay, but Sam wasn't too sure about the love story.

"I feel like Scarlett O'Hara from the movie." Caitlin tilted her head back dramatically like she was a celebrity. As they walked down the stairs together into the Rotunda lobby, she held out her hand to Sam. "Will you direct me to my carriage, sir?"

Sam blushed and awkwardly took her hand. Caitlin walked over and collapsed on one of the leather couches like she was about to faint. Derek cracked up on the bottom step.

"Quite a staircase, isn't it?" a voice called from the side of the room. Sam turned and saw a man dressed in a brown-and-burgundy uniform standing in the back of the room next to the gift shop. He had dark skin and a thick gray mustache.

"Sorry, we're just playing around," said Caitlin, letting go of Sam's hand and sitting up straight on the couch.

The man walked over to them with a smile. "That's okay, y'all stay as long as you want. How do you like the hotel?" He gestured across the Rotunda Lobby.

"It's awesome," said Derek.

"We're here for a wedding," explained Caitlin.

"Ah," said the man. "Beautiful place for a wedding."

Sam read the tag on the man's shirt. It said his name was *Moses*. He wore a hat similar to the valet's that had taken their car. Sam wondered if he was a bellman, like

Mr. Haskins had been. "Is your name really Moses? Like in the Bible?" He didn't remember meeting anyone with that name before.

"Yes it is, son. Moses T. Peterson, at your service." He leaned down closer with a toothy grin. "But you can call me Mo. That's what everyone else does. I'm Head Bellman here at The Jefferson."

Derek's ears perked up. "Hey, our neighbor used to be a bellman here too."

"A long time ago," said Sam.

Mo raised his eyebrows. "Is that right? What's your neighbor's name? I'll bet I know him."

"Mr. Haskins," answered Derek.

Mo laughed. "Jonas Haskins?"

Derek nodded.

"Why sure I know old Jonas. He's a crazy cat, that one. Haven't seen him in years. I think he was just leaving as I was starting out here." He took off his hat and scratched his head. "You tell old Jonas that Mo Peterson says hello. Will you do that?"

"Sure," said Derek.

Sam thought of Mr. Haskins' picture and looked around suspiciously. "You don't have any more alligators here, do you?"

"He's really nervous about the alligators," said Derek.

"Sam, that was a long time ago," said Caitlin. "Didn't you read the sign?"

"She's right," said Mo. "There really were alligators here, but that was even before my time. In fact, in the

22

old days, this corner over here was the hotel registration desk." He pointed to a bar area next to the Rotunda Lobby. "Folks used to bring containers of baby alligators now and then and leave them here at the front desk."

"Why would people have baby alligators?" asked Caitlin.

"Yeah, they're not exactly normal pets," said Derek.

Mo grinned. "Well, folks say that locals would get gators on vacation down in Florida and then bring them back home with them as pets."

"That's crazy," said Derek.

"Maybe so," continued Mo, "but after they got too big to live in sinks and bathtubs, folks would bring 'em here to the hotel."

Sam thought about having a pet alligator in his bathtub. That didn't sound like the kind of pet he'd enjoy having around. He looked at his feet and imagined baby alligators scurrying around like rats on the oriental rugs and marble floors. He looked up at Mo and tilted his head. "Really?"

Mo nodded. "That's right. Some of them ended up staying at the hotel." He pointed across the room toward the Jefferson statue. "They lived in long fountains that used to be in the Palm Court, up where you came in. Others were given away to zoos and the like."

Mo lowered his voice a bit and looked around as if to make sure no one else was listening. "What most folks don't know is that some of those little buggers never made it to the fountains or the zoos."

Sam opened his eyes wide. "They didn't?"

Mo shook his head.

"What happened to them?" asked Caitlin.

"Well..." Mo said, pausing like he wasn't sure if he should be talking about it or not. "I've been here a long time, and you see a lot of strange things at an old hotel."

"What kind of things?" asked Derek, moving closer so he could hear.

"Oh, strange noises, when the hotel is quiet. Even when the guests are gone or sleeping at night, the staff is still up, you know. Making sure everything's taken care of. Some folks say they've seen long-lost alligators walking around, descendants of a few lost baby gators that never made it to the registration desk. Folks say they slipped out of their cages and into passageways under the staircase here. There's drains and tunnels under there that lead beneath the basement and out to the city sewers."

"They lived under the stairs?" asked Derek.

Mo nodded. "Folks say they've lived down there for decades, like in the wild, undisturbed by people. Ah, most of the time they stay down there, not bothering anybody. But every once in a while, particularly in the winter like this when it gets cold, they come up out of the sewers and lie by the heat vents.

"Gators are cold blooded, ya know. They need to stay where it's warm. For the most part, Richmond's warm enough to keep 'em alive, but in those really cold parts of winter, the ice and the snow drive 'em up into the hotel.

Folks say you can hear their claws on the marble floors when they walk."

Sam could hardly breathe. Was Mo telling the truth?

"Did you ever see one?" asked Derek, his jaw hanging open.

"Maybe," smiled Mo. "Just once. I was cleaning out an air vent over near the Palm Court one evening. I was down on the floor, reaching for a bolt that I had dropped down the vent, when I heard a sound. Slow, but coming closer. Like nails, scratching the floor.

"Now I was kind of stuck there, mind you, my arm down the vent. I saw a shadow, coming toward me on the wall from around the corner. The sound on the marble grew louder and louder."

"What did you do?" asked Derek.

"Well, I was in a mighty awkward position, all laid out on the floor there. I could hardly breathe, let me tell ya. I tried not to make a sound, but my hand started shaking, and I dropped the bolt back into the vent. It clanged down into the duct work. I looked down to try to grab it, and when I looked back up, the shadow was gone."

"Didn't you go after it?" asked Derek.

"Sure, I stood up and walked around the corner in the hall, but whatever had been there was long gone." He chuckled. "They're fast little buggers, ya know."

"That could have been anything," said Caitlin. "You don't know it was an alligator."

"Maybe so," said Mo. "But I'm not the only one

who's seen things like that. Folks have also had things go missing that can't be explained."

"What's gone missing?" asked Sam, picturing himself being dragged away into the heating ducts by a rogue gator.

Mo grinned. "Oh, lots of different things. Shiny objects mostly: earrings, jewelry from people's rooms. Last year, a woman's miniature poodle, cute little thing, just vanished into thin air right here near this staircase."

Caitlin's mouth opened with surprise. "Vanished?"

"What happened to it?" asked Sam.

"Dunno," said Mo, shaking his head. "No trace of it anywhere."

A burst of static squawked from the radio on Mo's belt. "Whoops, that's my signal. Gotta go help a guest with some bags." He gave a quick half bow to the kids. "It's nice to meet y'all. I'm sure I'll see you around for the wedding."

Mo hustled off toward the lobby. Sam looked over at Caitlin. She looked skeptical.

"You don't believe him?" asked Sam.

"He's just trying to scare us," said Caitlin.

"What about the poodle?"

"Yeah, and the jewelry," added Derek.

"Maybe there's a thief," said Caitlin.

"Maybe it's the gators." Derek grinned.

"Please," said Sam, trying to convince himself. "There aren't any gators here at the hotel anymore." And he really, really hoped he was right.

CHAPTER FIVE

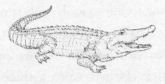

Mom and Dad walked into the Rotunda down the grand staircase from the Palm Court. They were laughing and chatting with a man and woman that Sam didn't recognize. Judging from the smile on Mom's face, it was Anita and her fiancé. Every time Mom had talked about seeing Anita for the past three weeks, her face had lit up with excitement.

A boy walked with them, trailing a few steps behind. Was that Nathan? He looked to be about Sam's age, maybe a year younger. He was short and skinny, so it was hard to tell. He had reddish-brown hair and a lot of freckles. He was holding a small video game player up very close to his face.

Sam had only seen Anita in old pictures from Mom's college days. Dad called them Mom's wild, party-girl years, although Sam had a hard time imagining his mom being anything close to a wild partier. A wild cleaner, maybe, but not a partier.

Anita looked a little different now, with short dark hair and a lot of makeup. Her fiancé was thin, like Nathan, but tall. He had a dark, but graying, beard trimmed short and dark-rimmed glasses that made him seem like someone trying to look cool. It reminded Sam of the guy who played Tony Stark in the Iron Man movies.

Mom introduced everyone. Anita's fiancé's name was Robert Wanderfelt. He spoke in a thick British accent, asking them to call him Robert, which felt weird to Sam, since he was used to calling grownups by their last names.

Sam initially misunderstood Anita, thinking she said Robert's last name was Wonderful. From then on he couldn't remember anything else, and after he mentioned it to Derek and Caitlin, they all started referring to Robert as Mr. Wonderful.

Nathan's name was easy to remember, but he didn't say anything. He just stared blankly down at his game.

Sam waved his hand. "How's it going?"

Nathan let out a deep sigh. "Classic," he said, with barely a glance away from his game.

Sam wasn't sure what that meant, but it didn't seem very friendly.

"Nathan, Sam said hello," Mr. Wonderful scolded, shaking his head. "Look at someone when they speak to you."

Nathan glanced up and down again faster than you could blink. "Hi, nice to meet you," he said, nose in his game again, before wandering over and sitting down on a couch.

"Nathan!" Robert barked, walking over to his son.

Anita shook her head and looked up at the others. "I'm sorry. Nathan's not handling all this very well. He's really a nice boy if you can ever pull him away from those video games. Robert had him in boarding school in England, but now we're all going to live happily together." She smiled weakly. "I hope."

Sam watched Nathan over on the couch. His dad seemed to be laying into him pretty hard. He thought of how Mr. Haskins was always saying that video games were rotting their brains. If he ever saw Nathan, he would have all the proof of that he needed.

"What is *that*?" Caitlin exclaimed, interrupting his thoughts. She pointed up to the Palm Court.

Everyone turned and looked across the room. Several men were carrying something large down the stairs and into the Rotunda. It looked like a rectangular box about the size of a small couch, and it was completely covered with a sheet.

"What is it?" asked Sam.

"I don't know, but I'll beat you there," said Derek, hustling past them.

"Boys, don't run!" yelled their mom.

They reached the men right as they set the box down

on the floor in the middle of the room. Everyone gathered around to see the mysterious arrival.

"What's under the blanket?" shouted Derek, unable to contain himself any longer.

Robert stepped forward and looked at Anita. He was grinning from ear to ear like he knew the answer to the secret. "This," he said, looking her in the eyes, "is a special present for you, love."

"For me?" Anita blushed and looked down at the sheet. "Robert, you shouldn't have."

"Well, let me clarify that," said Robert. "It's more like atmosphere, for our grand wedding."

"Oh," said Anita, her face turning more cautious. "Well that sounds...nice."

Sam figured it must be a new piece of furniture or something, although he wasn't sure why Robert would have brought it to the hotel. It was too big for a wedding dress...too small for a car...maybe it was a motorcycle!

Robert looked over at Derek. "You've heard the saying, 'When in Rome'?"

Derek shook his head. "I think you're on the wrong continent. This is Virginia."

Robert laughed. "Well, no matter. How about, 'When at the Jefferson'..." he nodded to the two men. They stepped up and pulled the sheet away, revealing a metal cage.

Inside the cage was an alligator!

"Whoa!" cried Derek.

It was about four feet long, but it wasn't moving.

Sam realized it must just be another statue. No one would let you bring a real alligator into the hotel. Even if you were Mr. Wonderful at The Jefferson.

"Oh my goodness, Robert!" exclaimed Anita, stepping back from the cage. "I think we need to talk a little more about what I find romantic."

Caitlin's eyes opened wide. "Is that real?"

Even Nathan looked up from his game, stepping toward the group to see the cage.

Sam smiled, leaning against the cage. "I'm not going to fall for that again. It's just a statue." He turned around to laugh at Derek and Caitlin.

"Sam—" started his dad, his eyes growing large.

As Sam turned back, the statue suddenly came alive.

CHAPTER SIX

T he alligator lunged toward Sam's hand, hitting the metal bars with a loud clang.

"Ahh!" Sam screamed, flailing backward until he fell onto one of the leather couches a good distance away from the cage.

Derek doubled over in laughter, his mouth open wide, pointing at Sam's face.

Robert grinned. "That's no statue, Sam. It's the real thing."

"Robert, really," said Anita. "You're getting a little carried away with this alligator thing." She turned to Mom, shaking her head. "He found vintage white heels for me to wear with my dress for the wedding. Made from alligator skin. Can you believe it?"

"That's awesome!" said Derek. "Who gets to have an alligator at their wedding?"

"I figured it would fit in perfectly here at The Jefferson, no?" said Robert.

Sam just nodded, still too startled to speak. He looked down and counted his fingers to make sure they were still attached. He couldn't believe he'd touched the cage.

Nathan stood next to the cage, eying the alligator carefully. "We're not taking that home, are we?" It was the most that Sam had heard him say. Nathan's voice had the same thick accent as his dad.

Robert placed a hand on Nathan's shoulder and shook his head. "No, no, nothing like that. It's just on loan from the zoo. I had to pull a few strings, let me tell you. But I'm sparing no expense for my Lovey Cakes." He reached over and pulled Anita into a tight hug.

Lovey Cakes? Derek made a face at Sam like he was going to puke. Sam and Caitlin tried to hold in their laughter.

Nathan's face tightened, and he wriggled free from his dad. He walked back over to the couch and picked up his device again.

Sam tried to breathe normally. He watched the alligator through the metal bars. It looked like it was staring back at him.

"Are you okay?" asked Caitlin, tapping Sam on the shoulder.

"Yeah."

"What's wrong?"

"Nothing," sighed Sam. "I just seem to be getting

scared by all the wrong things." He looked at the alligator cage out of the corner of his eye. "It's embarrassing."

Caitlin smiled. "Well I don't blame you. Who could have expected that they would bring a live alligator into the hotel? Even at The Jefferson."

A bell rang out from the Palm Court. Anita smiled and looked at her watch. "Oh, thank goodness." She whispered excitedly in Mom's ear.

"It's time for high tea!" exclaimed Anita.

Mom smiled and looked up in Sam's direction. "Oh, no," said Sam.

"What's wrong?" asked Caitlin.

"My mom has that look on her face."

"What look?"

"The one that means she's about to ask me to do something that I'm really not going to like."

* * *

"PLEASE PASS THE SUGAR CUBES."

Sam rolled his eyes as he handed the crystal bowl of white and brown sugar cubes to Caitlin. He refused to look over at his mom at the next table. She was in a deep conversation with Anita, seemingly not concerned about subjecting him to a tea party.

This was terrible. What was 'high tea' anyhow?

He looked across at Caitlin. She seemed to be enjoying herself. She was really excited about being in this fancy old hotel.

"Isn't this glamorous?" she giggled. "Just like walking on the staircase." She flashed a wide smile like she was having her picture taken. "I feel like a movie star."

Sam groaned. He didn't usually mind hanging out with Caitlin. Just not like this. And especially not when Derek was allowed to go with Dad to Robert's suite instead. That was totally unfair! Derek rubbed it in too, of course, making a big deal about not having to get dressed up and sit with a girl. He said it "wasn't his cup of tea." What a jerk.

And then there was Nathan-the-grump. He was sitting at their table too, although you'd hardly notice since he was still playing his video game. Sam and Caitlin had tried to talk to him, but he only offered one-word answers. He'd barely looked at them the whole time.

"Do you drink a lot of tea in England?" Caitlin asked.

"Sometimes," said Nathan.

"Do you like it?"

"Nah."

That was how it went, until Nathan pushed his chair back from the table and stood up. "I have to use the loo," he said, walking away.

"The what?" Sam couldn't understand some of the things Nathan and Robert said with their accent. He thought that they spoke English over there, but maybe not.

Caitlin shrugged. "So, I was reading some of the

history about this place on the displays in the glass cases downstairs."

"Uh, huh," Sam grunted, not really paying attention to what she was saying. He was still sulking about being there.

"It said that the hotel was built by Lewis Ginter," Caitlin continued, ignoring Sam's sour attitude. "Isn't that cool?"

"Awesome," sighed Sam, staring up at the light coming through the stained glass windows in the ceiling. It reflected off the top of the head on the Thomas Jefferson statue that rose out of the Palm Court lobby.

"You *have* been to Lewis Ginter Botanical Gardens, haven't you?" Caitlin never seemed to run out of energy when talking about something she'd learned. "It's one of my favorite places. Last year I went into the greenhouse for the butterfly exhibit, and three monarchs landed right on my arm. My mom said that if you touch a monarch's wing, it can rub off their—" Caitlin stopped mid-sentence as a waitress placed a small plate of pastries on their table.

Sam suddenly snapped out of his haze and admired the tasty-looking plate. It smelled delicious. "What are those?" he asked, pointing to a round treat that looked like a biscuit with flecks of color peppered throughout.

Caitlin picked one up with her fingers and placed it on her plate. "You've never had a scone before? Mmm, they're good. You should try one."

Sam forgot about being annoyed and smiled. They

certainly looked good. He grabbed one and took a quick bite. Blueberry. He loved blueberry. He looked over at Mom. Maybe this wasn't so bad after all.

As he chewed his scone, he spied Mo walking out from behind the front desk toward the Grand Staircase. "There's something suspicious about him," he said, nodding in Mo's direction.

"What do you mean?" asked Caitlin. "He seemed friendly earlier."

"Too friendly, if you ask me," said Sam. "Maybe he's the one responsible for all the missing things."

Caitlin chuckled. "That's just how people in the South are, Sam."

"How, suspicious?"

"No! Friendly. Don't be so pessimistic." She took a sip of tea from her china cup. "Besides, I thought you said it was the alligators that stole everything?" She giggled.

Sam felt his face turning red, so he took another bite of scone and wiped his mouth on the cloth napkin. "One or the other," he mumbled through a full bite.

"Pardon me, sir, but might I have a bit of tea?" a voice called from behind them in a corny British accent. Sam turned around and saw Derek standing there with a grin on his face. Reaching over Sam's shoulder, he snatched the last blueberry scone.

"Hey!" cried Sam.

"Mmm, thanks," Derek said through a big bite. "I'm starving."

"Please...help yourself," said Caitlin.

"Thank you, Caitlin," Derek looked down at Sam. "See, little brother, that's called southern hospitality. You should try it sometime."

"How about I show you some northern aggression?" Sam stood and raised his fist.

Derek leaped back nimbly before Sam could reach him, bumping into Nathan returning to the table. Nathan sat down, then looked up at Sam with a cross expression. "Where's my video game?"

"Your what?" said Sam.

"My game, I left it here on the table. It's gone. What did you do with it?" His voice was high pitched now.

"Nathan, we didn't touch your game," said Caitlin. "We've been sitting here the whole time."

"Eating scones," mumbled Derek, with his mouth still packed.

Sam scowled at him for taking the last one.

Nathan's face was getting redder and redder. "Well somebody took it!"

CHAPTER SEVEN

Sam's dad and Mr. Wonderful walked up to the table. "I know you two wouldn't be causing trouble, right?" said Dad.

"Dad!" yelled Nathan, grabbing Robert's arm. "He stole my game." Nathan pointed right at Sam.

Sam felt his heart beating faster. "What?" He looked up at his dad. "I didn't do anything, honest."

"We were just sitting here," said Caitlin.

"Nathan, where was the last place you had it?" said Robert. He shook his head. "Maybe it's for the best. Honestly, that's the only thing you ever do, playing that bloody game."

Nathan stomped his foot. "It is not. I went to the loo, and when I came back, it was gone."

"The zoo?" said Derek. "Well that's probably where you left it. Maybe it's next to the alligators."

Nathan just scowled at him.

Mom walked over and patted Derek's shoulder. "Not the zoo, honey, the loo. It's what the British call the bathroom."

Sam nearly choked as he sipped his tea. That made more sense now, but he still didn't know where Nathan's video game had gone.

"Why don't you look in the restroom," said Anita. "Maybe you left it there."

Nathan grumbled something under his breath and stormed away from the table.

Sam looked up at his parents. "Honest, I didn't take it."

"Okay," said Mom, "I believe you. But as you can see, that game is important to Nathan. If you do see it, let us know right away."

A waitress stared at their table. "Are you done with your tea, miss?"

"We were just finishing," said Caitlin, placing her napkin on the table.

Sam's mom looked at her watch. "There's just enough time to go for a swim before we have to get changed for the rehearsal and dinner, if you want to."

"That's right, there's an indoor pool down the hall from our room," said Derek. "Can we go?" Mom nodded and Derek bounded off toward the elevator.

"Do you think Nathan would like to swim?" asked Mom.

"No," said Robert, "I think he can probably use some quiet time."

Swimming actually sounded fun to Sam. Better than sitting here playing tea party and getting yelled at by Nathan. Even if there were scones. He looked at Caitlin. "Can you come?"

"I don't know..." said Caitlin. "Wait! Yes, my dad packed my suit just in case. I just remembered!"

"Sweet," said Sam. Caitlin was a great swimmer.

"Meet you there in a few minutes?" said Caitlin.

Sam nodded.

"Just keep an eye on the water," said Mr. Wonderful.

"Why?" asked Sam.

"In case there are any lurking alligators," Mr. Wonderful replied with a smile.

Anita elbowed him in the ribs. "Robert! Let's not scare the boy any more than you already have. Why did you bring that beast in here in the first place?"

Robert puffed up his chest like he was proud of himself. "Beast? Please. That alligator belongs here." He pointed into the hotel. "It's part of the history. They should be glad that someone like me helped them out."

Anita shook her head and walked over to where Mom was standing. "He makes me wonder sometimes."

CHAPTER EIGHT

The elevator doors opened with a ding and Caitlin stepped out. She waved at Sam and Derek who were standing in the Palm Court.

"Hey," said Sam.

"That was refreshing," said Caitlin, her hair still wet and pulled back from swimming. They'd played a long game of Marco Polo in the water, which consisted mostly of Derek trying to dunk Sam's head under the water while pretending that his eyes were still closed.

"I didn't know you were such a good swimmer, Caitlin," said Derek.

She smiled. "I'm on the swim team."

"Maybe she could give you lessons, Sam."

Sam tried to hold in his anger. Just once he wished that they could hang out without Derek making fun of him. "I can swim just fine, thank you, when you're not pushing me under."

Derek shrugged. "What can I say, I don't know my own strength." He glanced around. "So where's the rehearsal dinner? I'm starving."

Caitlin pointed across the room to a marble doorway with black iron gates on both sides. Just like everything else in the hotel, it looked very elegant. Between him and the restaurant was the life-size Thomas Jefferson statue. Sam stared up at it. Perched up on the pedestal, it was much taller than he was.

"He lost his head once, you know," a voice said behind him. Sam turned around to see Mo. That was the second time he'd snuck up on them like that. "Oh, hey Mo," said Sam.

"What do you mean he lost his head once?" asked Caitlin.

"Thomas Jefferson or the statue?" said Derek.

Mo smiled. "The statue, thank goodness."

"It looks connected to me," said Derek.

Sam looked closer at the top of the statue. There certainly didn't seem to be any cracks from where he stood.

"Well, it was repaired, as you can see. But it was damaged in the great fire." Mo nodded. "Yes siree. Way back in 1901 there was a huge fire, nearly wiped the place out. Just six years after the hotel opened. They had to do a big renovation. It shut the hotel down for years."

"Was anyone killed?" asked Caitlin.

"No," said Mo. "Thankfully the only casualty was Mr. Jefferson here."

43

"What happened to him? I mean the statue," said Sam.

Mo stepped closer to the statue. "Well, crews came in to rescue the statue. They wrapped it up in mattresses and carried it out into the street."

Sam imagined trying to carry the big statue out of the building without a forklift. "It looks heavy."

Mo chuckled. "Must have been. Because in all the commotion, they dropped it and the head broke clear off."

"Oh no!" cried Caitlin.

"I bet that guy got fired," said Derek. He nudged Sam in the ribs. "Get it? Fired...because of the fire?"

Sam shook his head slowly. His brother could be so lame sometimes. He turned back to Mo. "But they fixed it?"

Mo nodded again. "Yep. They saved it. The original sculptor, Mr. Valentine, kept the head and eventually returned the repaired statue for the reopening six years later."

"Wow," whistled Derek, looking around. "It's a good thing they saved this place. It's pretty cool."

"Yes it is, boys," said Mo with a wide smile. "When it opened one hundred and twenty years ago, it was one of the finest hotels in the country. Electric elevators, palm trees from South America, Turkish Baths... And it isn't too shabby today. I'm a lucky man to be working at such a famous place."

"Turkey Baths?" asked Derek, turning his head.

Sam elbowed his brother in the ribs and looked back at Mo. "So what do you think happened to that lady's poodle and the jewelry you told us about?"

"Yeah," said Derek, "do you really think it was the gators?"

"Ha!" cackled Mo, grinning. "I think I may have played a bit too much on you youngsters' imaginations. Mrs. Peterson is always telling me that I need to keep my mouth shut." Mo considered his own words for a moment, but then bent down toward them with a big grin. "But you know, if it was the gators that stole everything, they might have taken it down into the passageways that run beneath the hotel."

"What passageways?" Nathan asked, walking up to them. Sam noticed he still didn't have his video game. He seemed more interested in what was going on without it.

Mo laughed. "Got your attention too, did I? Well, you know that fancy staircase over in the Rotunda?"

"Yeah," said Derek.

"Legend says that around the back of it was an entrance to a passageway. It was covered up after the renovations and the fire. The passageway leads down below the cellar. Supposedly there are tunnels that go halfway around the city underground."

"There are?" asked Sam. This sounded a bit like a tall tale.

"That's what they say," said Mo, straightening up. "But who knows for sure. There's always rumors of all kinds of things in old buildings like this. I don't get paid to snoop around in the sewers."

"What do you mean they're bloody gone?" a voice yelled across the room.

Everyone looked up to see Anita and Robert walking out of the elevator. Robert's face was red, and he was gesturing with his arms. Anita was trying to quiet him down, moving him away from everyone's stares.

"Uh-oh," said Mo. "Looks like there might be some trouble. Excuse me, kids."

"I wonder what's going on," said Caitlin.

"Looks like Mr. Wonderful isn't feeling so wonderful at the moment," said Derek. Mom and Dad walked toward the kids with Anita and Robert. Mom had a concerned look on her face.

"What's the matter, Mom?" asked Sam.

She cast a hesitant glance at Dad. Before she could answer, Robert jumped in. His face looked like it was about to explode. "I'll tell you what's wrong," he shouted, his voice echoing off the stained glass ceiling. "The wedding rings have been stolen!"

CHAPTER NINE

The room buzzed with confusion over Robert's announcement that the rings were missing.

"What?" exclaimed Derek.

Sam tried to take it all in.

"How could that happen?" asked Caitlin.

Anita looked like she was about to burst into tears. "We had the rings upstairs in our suite. I had them in a separate jewelry box on the table next to the vanity. I'm just sure of it."

"Nothing else was touched, mind you," said Robert. "Not my watch, my wallet, nothing. And there were these strange brown streaks. They looked like mud on the carpet, leading from the hall. How can you explain that?" He narrowed his eyes and glared over at the front desk. "This is not the type of service that I expect from a hotel of this prestige."

Anita leaned against Robert's shoulder. "I need to sit

down. I'm not feeling well." She headed toward the restaurant.

"I'll come with you, Anita," said Mom. She tapped Dad's arm. "Honey, go see if you can calm Robert down." Dad nodded and walked with Robert into the restaurant a step or two behind Mom and Anita. Mo and the hotel manager shuffled by, concerned looks on their faces. Mo was talking into his radio. This wasn't good.

Derek grimaced. "Well, there goes the wedding."

"Poor Anita," said Caitlin. "She's so upset."

"It looks like Robert's the one that's upset about it to me," said Derek.

"He just wants the wedding to be perfect," said Nathan, in a cross voice. He stepped up into Sam's face. "You probably took them, just like you stole my game!" He shoved Sam toward the statue.

"Hey!" Sam stumbled backward and fell.

"Don't push him," said Caitlin. "He didn't take your stupid video game." She reached out to help Sam up. "And he certainly didn't steal any wedding rings."

Nathan scowled and started walking toward the restaurant and his dad. "We'll see," he called over his shoulder.

Sam stood up without Caitlin's help and frowned. He turned to Derek who was just watching with a goofy grin. "Thanks a lot for helping."

"I was standing by," said Derek, "but your girl had it covered."

"He's kind of a jerk," said Caitlin, shaking her head at Nathan's back.

Sam tended to agree. Some people liked to take things out on others when they got mad. He couldn't understand what had made Nathan so upset. He looked back at Caitlin. "What do you think happened to the rings?"

"You mean, you didn't take them?" asked Derek.

Sam gave his brother a disgusted look.

Caitlin smacked Derek's arm. "Stop it! Be serious. The wedding is tomorrow and they need the rings. It's important."

"So who took them?" said Sam. He tried to think about who could have done it. He looked across the room where Mo was still talking on his radio. "Mo probably has access to the rooms. It could have been him."

Caitlin shook her head. "No way. He's too nice. Why would he want to steal wedding rings anyway?"

"Maybe he needs the money," suggested Sam. "I haven't seen them, but I bet Mr. Wonderful's rings are pretty wonderful."

Derek folded his arms across his chest. "Well, I still think that Sam is a reasonable suspect, but if it's not him, you're forgetting something pretty obvious."

"What?" asked Sam.

"Didn't you hear Mr. Wonderful? There were dark streaks of mud on the carpet from the hallway. It was an alligator!"

"Derek..." said Caitlin.

Derek kept a straight face. "What? You heard Mo. They live in the sewers and the passageways. The cold weather drives them up into the hotel... have you looked outside? It's winter."

Sam cocked his head to the side. "Yeah, but..."

"First they ate the poodle," Derek continued, his eyes growing wide. "Next was Nathan's video game. Now the wedding rings."

He paused dramatically and looked back and forth between them. "Which one of us will be next?"

"Knock it off, will you?" said Sam, looking away from his brother. All his life, Derek had been trying to scare him. It was tiring.

Derek pointed toward the staircase into the Rotunda. "You know, there's only one way to find out. We have to track down the reptile lair. Maybe there are alligators living all over the city. Maybe they're stealing things left and right and nobody knows about it. Maybe—"

"Derek!" shouted Caitlin. "We get it."

Sam shook his head. "No way, Derek. I've had enough alligators."

Derek grinned. "Come on. You know my plans always work out to be something fantastic." He tilted his head and made another cocky expression. "It's a special gift, Sam."

"You're special, all right," Sam muttered, as his brother walked off toward the staircase. "But not the way you're thinking."

"Just forget about him," Caitlin said.

Sam thought back to the rings. "What do you think about the muddy streaks in the carpet? It couldn't really be from an alligator, could it?"

"Alligators don't just slither up to a table, chomp down on a jewelry box, and leave a trail of muddy footprints, Sam."

"Actually, alligators don't slither. That's more like snakes. Alligators walk." He remembered that from a Nature Channel show he'd seen.

Caitlin waved her hand. "You know what I mean." She paused, then said, "Maybe it was Nathan."

Sam shook his head. "What about his video game? Did he steal his own stuff, too?"

Caitlin smirked. "No, that has an easy explanation."

"It does?"

"Sure, we all know you stole that one, Sam!" She giggled and ran.

"Hey!" Sam exclaimed, chasing her out of the Palm Court and down the staircase into the Rotunda.

Nathan must not have stayed with his dad in the restaurant long, because he was standing next to the alligator cage in the middle of the room. The sheet was draped over it again, but a few inches of the cage's bars showed at the bottom. Nathan was crouched down and staring through the bars, a curious look on his face. As Sam and Caitlin approached, he jerked his hand away from the latch at the front of the cage.

"What are you doing?" asked Sam.

"Nothing..." said Nathan.

"You'd better watch your fingers," said Caitlin. "You saw what almost happened to Sam."

"Don't worry about me," responded Nathan. "I'm not that stupid."

Sam frowned but tried to ignore Nathan. He supposed that he'd be feeling pretty upset if his dad was marrying someone new and moving them all across the ocean. It was a pretty big deal.

As he walked by the cage, Sam bent down and took a quick glance. He saw the alligator's scaly legs and protruding claws under the edge of the sheet. He bounced back up. That was enough for him. He didn't need any more chances of losing a finger now that he knew the beast was real.

He joined Caitlin over in a corner of the room to the right of the staircase. It looked like a mini museum with display cases and pictures of the hotel from years ago on the wall. "What are you looking at?"

"I'm reading these old newspapers about Lewis Ginter." She pointed down into a display. "Did you know that at one point, he was the wealthiest man in the South?"

"Wow," said Sam. He tried to imagine being the richest man anywhere. "That's richer than Mr. Wonderful." He could buy a lot of basketball shoes with money like that.

"Oh my gosh."

"What?"

"Look at this," said Caitlin. "He died just two years after the hotel was finished."

"That stinks," said Sam, looking around the Rotunda. "He never even got to enjoy this place." He thought about what Mo said about the secret passageway. "At least he didn't see the fire."

Caitlin nodded. "He probably rolled over in his grave."

Sam wasn't sure what that meant, but he'd heard his grandma use that expression before.

"Hey, look." Caitlin pointed to another old picture. "I'll bet you've *seen* his grave."

Sam leaned in to see. It did look familiar. "Is that St. John's Church?" He'd seen George Wythe's grave there once. That was probably it.

"Nope," said Caitlin.

Sam read the caption under the picture.

"*Lewis Ginter was laid to rest in Hollywood Cemetery, in a grand mausoleum overlooking the James River.*"

He looked up. "Oh yeah. That's where we saw the Confederate Ghosts." He shivered thinking about watching the notorious biker gang from behind some tombstones. "I don't know if we saw *his* grave though."

"Maybe you just didn't realize it," said Caitlin. "That happens to me a lot. There's so much history in Richmond. My mom says that's what makes it fun to learn about," said Caitlin. "You can appreciate all those things when you see them and again when you realize you saw something important you didn't even know about."

Sam nodded, looking back out at the room. He liked history too, but Caitlin took things to another level.

He watched Derek walking back and forth around the staircase. Sam walked over, following him around the left side. Derek was staring at the walls.

"Did you find anything yet, Sherlock?"

"Don't be so negative, Sam. If we always gave up when *you* wanted, we'd never have *any* adventures." Derek walked back to the front of the stairs. "Let's see... Mo said the passageway was covered up after the fire. Maybe the entrance is under a loose floor tile. I think I saw that in a movie once..." He raised up his foot and stomped hard on the ground. The noise echoed loudly around the Rotunda. Several people on the balcony stopped talking and turned toward them.

"Derek!" hissed Sam.

"Stop," said Caitlin. "You can't do that at a hotel like this."

Derek grimaced and waved to the people in the balcony. "Sorry."

Sam stepped past Derek and his stomping. "He said it was under the staircase. Maybe it's in the wall." He gently touched the wall along the side of the staircase, but didn't see any opening.

"Here, let me try," said Derek, pulling his arm back and aiming his fist at the wall.

"No!" shouted Sam. His yell echoed off the marble archways and ceiling all around them.

Derek dropped his arm and laughed hysterically. The

people on the balcony looked down at them again. Sam covered his face with his hand, his cheeks burning.

Caitlin waved meekly up at the people. "Sorry!"

"Sam, you need to chillax," said Derek.

"Chillax?" said Caitlin. "What's that?"

"It's when you combine 'chill' and 'relax'." Derek spread his arms wide. "Chillax. It's a new word. I just invented it."

"You did not," said Sam, moving out of view of the people in the balcony. Derek never ceased to amaze him with his weirdness.

"You're welcome to use it, if you want," said Derek, grinning.

"You know," said Caitlin, walking under the staircase, "I do remember my dad saying that there is a tunnel system that runs under the city like Mo said. He told me about it after one of his photo shoots over at the Capitol building. I don't know if it extends all the way over here to The Jefferson, though."

"Maybe it is just a legend," said Derek. "Or Mo got confused. He's probably getting senile like Mr. Haskins."

"Be nice," said Caitlin.

Sam agreed with his brother on this one. "Wouldn't you think Mo would know for sure if it were real? He does work here."

"Maybe he just forgot. He's kind of old," said Caitlin.

"See, I told you. He's crazy as crackers," said Derek.

Caitlin laughed. "I thought you liked him?"

"I do," said Derek, "but that doesn't mean that he's not crazy."

Derek stood next to the bottom step and stared up to the top of the grand staircase. "I wonder if you could sled down these."

"I don't think so," said Sam.

Derek grinned wide. "Yeah, but it would be awesome if you could, wouldn't it?"

"I guess..." said Caitlin.

"Kids, come on," a voice called from the top of the staircase. It was Mom. The rest of the wedding party was gathering to walk through the ceremony rehearsal. "We're about to start."

"Come on," said Sam. "The passageway, if it even exists, will have to wait."

"I'm going to go ask Mo if he has any sleds," said Derek.

Caitlin frowned as Derek bounded off. "But wait—" she started, before Sam put his hand up.

"Don't waste your time," said Sam. "It's not worth it. Trust me."

CHAPTER TEN

After the rehearsal, everyone walked up past the Palm Court and into the main restaurant. A side room had been arranged with three round tables, each with eight chairs. His parents were seated at one table next to Robert and Anita. There was an older couple next to Anita who Sam figured must be her parents. At the second table were several couples about his parents' age. Sam didn't recognize any of them.

Everyone was dressed very formally; the men were in suits and ties, the women in fancy dresses. Sam looked down at his attire of khakis and a collared shirt. He guessed that he'd got off easy this time not having to wear a suit.

Nathan was already seated at the third table. Sam noticed small white cards with names printed on them next to each place setting of fine china.

"Looks like we're all sitting together again," said

Caitlin. She gave a wave to her dad who was standing in the corner of the room taking pictures of the dinner. It seemed like Mr. Wonderful wanted every moment of the weekend documented. Sam's mom had recommended that Anita hire Mr. Murphy as a wedding photographer. When Anita learned that Caitlin and Sam were friends, she offered to let Caitlin join them at the dinner. It was pretty nice.

Nathan looked up at them and groaned. "Classic."

Sam reached for the pitcher of sweet tea in the center of the table, but before he could pick it up, a waiter scurried over and poured a glass for him. "Thank you," Sam said.

The waiter left, then returned to their table, placing a white cloth napkin in each of their laps. Except for Caitlin. Hers was black.

Sam scrunched his eyebrows. That seemed strange. "Are black napkins for girls?"

The waiter chuckled. "No, no," he said in a thick accent. "Not because she's a lady." The waiter pointed to Caitlin. "For the dark."

"The dark?" Sam was confused. "We're going to eat in the dark?" What was he talking about?

Caitlin smiled. "I think he means that since my dress is a dark blue color, he gave me a dark-colored napkin. So it blends in."

The waiter nodded. "Yes, yes."

"Ohh," said Sam. "I get it now." The rest of them

were wearing lighter-colored pants, so they got white napkins. He felt stupid again.

"Don't you ever eat out in this country?" asked Nathan.

"Yeah, jeez, Sam," joked Derek. "You need to be more cultured."

Sam shot his brother a nasty look.

The waiter handed out large rectangular menus to each of them. There were no pages to turn. Everything was printed on one side in fancy lettering.

"Lee Mary?" said Derek, trying to pronounce the name of the restaurant at the top. "Who's Lee Mary?"

Caitlin giggled. "Lemaire, silly," she said, pronouncing the second part so that it rhymed with hair. "It's French."

Sam smirked at his brother. "Who's not very cultured now, Derek?"

"Right," answered Derek. "I was just testing you. I wonder what it means?"

Their waiter appeared at the table from the side of the room. It was like they had their own personal butler.

"Lemaire," said the waiter, "is named after Etienne Lemaire."

"Who was he?" asked Derek.

"Etienne Lemaire was the maître d'hôtel to Thomas Jefferson while he was president."

"The what?" asked Derek.

Nathan shook his head again. "You know, the maître d'," he said, pronouncing it almost like 'Major Dee'.

"Uh, huh..." replied Derek. "What does that mean?"

"A maître d' is the person at a restaurant who is in charge of the waiters and reservations and stuff like that," explained Caitlin. "I guess naming the restaurant after Lemaire makes sense since the hotel was named after Jefferson."

"That's pretty cool," said Sam, scanning the menu. He tried to find words that he understood so no one had to explain anything else to him. The menu seemed to be in English, but just barely.

As Sam studied the menu, a team of waiters appeared, placing plates of leafy green salads around the table. He realized the menu was the same for everyone. It said the salad was the first course.

While Sam tried to decide which fork to use for his salad, one of the grownups he didn't know started tapping on their glass with a spoon. Everyone stopped talking and stared up at the first table.

"What are they doing?" asked Nathan.

Caitlin smiled. "I think that means they should kiss."

"Who should kiss?" said Nathan, looking around.

"The bridal couple," replied Caitlin. "Although they usually don't do that until after the wedding, at the reception. I was at my cousin Tracy's wedding last summer, and people were doing that all the time. It was funny."

Sam grimaced. He didn't see how a lot of kissing could be funny. More like gross.

Robert and Anita looked up from their conversations

and laughed. Robert dramatically leaned in toward Anita and kissed her softly on the cheek. "More to come tomorrow. Not to worry!" he said.

The grownups all laughed, but Nathan's face turned red. "That's a stupid thing to do."

Caitlin frowned at Nathan and looked at the rest of them. "I hope they are able to relax, even with the wedding rings missing."

"What are they going to do if they can't find the rings? Does that mean that they can't get married?" said Sam. He didn't know much about weddings, but it seemed like you must need wedding rings.

Caitlin shook her head. "Rings are just a symbol. They can still get married without them. Or they could just use something else." She nodded back toward the first table. Mr. Wonderful was standing and about to say something.

"First of all," Robert began, "I'd like to thank you all for coming. It is a privilege to see so many old friends and family." He gestured to Mom and Dad and the other grownups.

"You know, I'm very proud of all that I've accomplished in my life. I've never let an opportunity get away from me, never rested when there was something still to be gained. It's an honor to be here at The Jefferson, which they tell me has served as host to thirteen American presidents, Frank Sinatra, Charles Lindbergh, and many more."

"Like Elvis!" shouted Derek from their table.

Everyone turned around and stared at him. Derek gave a weak wave and showed his teeth in a silly smile. "It's true..." he said more quietly.

Sam could see Dad close his eyes while Mom just shook her head.

Mr. Wonderful chuckled. "Thank you, Derek."

Derek nodded back at him.

Robert paused and looked over at Nathan. "When my son and I lost Charlotte five years ago, I was devastated. I let my work take over my life. I didn't think I would love again. But then I met the most amazing woman at a fundraiser in Boston. Seventeen trips across the pond later, here we are today."

He took Anita's hand in his and smiled. "Sweetheart, I know that I may be a bit eccentric, talk too loud, and let my emotions get the best of me. I know that everything might not be perfect. We may not have rings tomorrow to adorn our fingers. But what I hold for you in my heart sparkles more than any diamond. It shines brighter than any band of gold. I love you, Anita."

Everyone around the room ah-ed and clapped as Robert bent down and gave Anita another light kiss. This time on the lips.

Sam looked around his table as he took a long sip of his sweet tea. Nathan seemed miserable. Sam hadn't known that Nathan's mom had died. It probably made things even harder for him, although Anita seemed like a nice lady.

"Wasn't that romantic?" gushed Caitlin. She seemed to be staring at Sam with big puppy dog eyes. Yikes.

Derek kicked Sam's leg underneath the table. A big grin filled his face.

"Uh," said Sam, blushing. "Yeah. That was really nice." And it was, he just didn't know what Caitlin was all smiley about.

"See," said Caitlin. "I told you weddings weren't just about rings."

Sam was getting tired of talking about weddings. And he needed to get away from Caitlin. She was acting weird. "Excuse me," he said. "I have to go to the bathroom."

"You mean the loo?" joked Derek, nudging Nathan in the chair next to him.

Nathan frowned and stared back toward the head table. It was like he was shooting darts at Anita through his eyes.

"Right," said Sam. "Whatever. I'll be back."

He made his way out through the Palm Court to the bathroom.

When he returned to his seat, the main course had arrived. Caitlin smiled at him. "Derek wanted to eat your dinner, but I didn't let him."

"That's nice of you," answered Sam, cutting his juicy steak with his knife. His stomach growled. This looked delicious. He hadn't realized how hungry he was.

"Look, there's Mo," said Derek.

Sam turned and saw Mo walking over to Robert and Anita's table. "I wonder what he's up to?"

"Maybe he found the rings," said Caitlin.

Sam raised his eyebrow suspiciously. "Oh, I think he might know where to find them…"

"I thought they didn't need rings?" asked Derek, smiling.

"They don't… but it would still be nice," said Caitlin.

Mo bent down and whispered something into Mr. Wonderful's ear. Robert's mouth opened wide, and he dropped his fork onto his plate with a clatter. He slowly rose from his chair, his face as white as a ghost.

"Everyone…can I have everyone's attention please." The room quieted and the guests all stared back up at him.

"Another toast?" whispered Derek. "Geez, enough is enough, Mr. Romance."

Sam chuckled in between bites.

"There's no need to panic," Mr. Wonderful said, looking a bit panicked, "but I'm afraid that we have a bit of a situation."

Sam stopped chewing and listened intently. What was going on?

"The, uh…" he stammered. "My…um…"

"The alligator is missing!" interrupted Mo.

CHAPTER ELEVEN

A few things happened at once after Mo announced that the alligator was missing. First, Anita fainted, her head falling smack into her mashed potatoes. For a change, Robert looked bewildered, like he didn't know what to do. Sam bet that Mr. Wonderful didn't have a lot of wild animals roaming about in his business. Mom was helping Anita get back into her chair while wiping the potatoes from her hair. Dad was talking to Anita's parents, trying to explain what was happening. Everyone seemed to be talking at the same time.

The hotel manager ran into the room and began talking excitedly to Mo. His arms were waving and he was sweating. Sam wasn't sure whose idea it was to allow Mr. Wonderful to bring the alligator into the hotel, but he bet they were regretting it right about now. The hotel manager grabbed Mo's radio out of his hand, speaking quickly into it as he ran out of the room again.

Derek sat there with a wild grin on his face, watching everything unfold around him. Caitlin reached over and held Sam's hand. He wasn't sure if she did it because she was scared or because *he* looked scared.

Derek tugged on Sam's arm and motioned him and Caitlin into the hallway. Sam finished off his remaining piece of steak with two big bites. Nathan just sat in his seat, staring at the commotion all around them like he was in a trance.

They walked through the Palm Court to the staircase and the entrance to the Rotunda. Sam scanned the floor for any sign of the escaped reptile. This seemed like a bad idea. "I'm not going down there."

Derek scoffed. "Chicken."

Caitlin shook her head. "No, I'm with Sam. There's no telling where it could have gone. Real alligators are dangerous."

Sam's attention drifted toward the middle of the room. The sheet was off of the alligator cage. The door was open. The alligator was really gone.

"Be careful, kids," warned the hotel manager, brushing past them with three more uniformed staff. They poked around the edges of the room, looking behind couches and curtains.

"I'll bet it's long gone," said Derek. "It got a taste of freedom and made a run for it."

"Where do you think it would go?" asked Caitlin.

"Who knows?" Derek pointed toward the back entrance. "It could have gone outside, down into the sewers. It could be in the James River by now, halfway to the Chesapeake Bay."

"Sure," said Sam. Derek had an "active imagination," as his teachers would say. But even without one, it was easy to be nervous. Sam thought back to when Mr. Haskins first showed them the picture of the alligator in the hotel. He remembered thinking that he would never go to a place where live alligators ran free. He glanced around him and gulped. Too late.

Mom and Dad, and the others from the rehearsal dinner, filed out of the restaurant and walked toward them.

Nathan pointed at Sam. "There he is!"

Sam touched his chest. "Me?"

"You went to the loo right before they noticed the alligator missing," exclaimed Nathan. "I know you let him out, just like you stole my game."

Sam felt his heart beating faster. The only thing that got him more stressed than dangerous situations was having someone accuse him of something he hadn't done. "I didn't even go near the cage," he protested. "I just went to the bathroom."

"Nathan," said Anita, "let's not go accusing people for no reason. I'm sure Sam didn't let the alligator out of the cage."

"Yeah, why would he even do that?" said Caitlin.

Sam shook his head. "I wouldn't. Honest. I swear." He looked up at his mom and dad with pleading eyes.

"If Sam says he didn't touch the cage, then he didn't

touch the cage," said Dad. "He had no reason to let it out."

"Yeah, he's scared to death of alligators," added Derek. "He won't even go near the cage."

Mr. Wonderful nodded. "Yes, that's a good point." He looked down at Nathan. "I'm sure there's a perfectly reasonable explanation, son."

Caitlin looked at Nathan. "You were the one touching the latch before dinner. We saw you. Maybe you let it out."

"It wasn't me," said Nathan. He glared at Sam and stormed off to the elevator.

Sam let out a deep breath.

"I think everyone should go to their rooms," announced the hotel manager. "That's the safest place for you all. Rest assured, we'll do a diligent search. I'm sure all will be accounted for by morning."

Mom looked at her watch. "It's already late, you kids should get to bed soon."

"But what if it's in our room?" asked Sam. "We'd be trapped."

"Then you're dead," said Derek, making a cutting motion across his neck with his finger. "Nice knowing you. Can I have your baseball cards?"

CHAPTER TWELVE

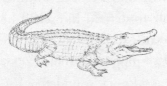

"**D**erek," scolded their dad. "That's enough. We'll check the room first. Don't worry, Sam. I'll walk you up."

Mom nodded. "I'm going to help Anita get squared away first. She's had a rough day." She pointed over to the restaurant. "Here comes your father, Caitlin. Looks like we all left him without a rehearsal dinner to photograph."

Sam followed his dad and Derek up to their hotel room. It was a *deluxe* room, which meant it had a balcony with a great view of the city. Right now, Sam would have been happy with a smaller room since it would give a lurking alligator fewer places to hide.

Thankfully, it was an adjoining room, which meant Mom and Dad's room was connected to theirs. A door in-between could be opened or locked from both sides. When they'd arrived, Sam and Derek had fun knocking on both sides of the door and pretending that they were barging into someone else's hotel room by surprise. The door was closed now, but Sam knew that it was unlocked if he needed to make a quick getaway.

Sam sat down and glanced around his bed. How would he be able to defend himself if he fell asleep? He pictured the alligator slithering up the side of his bed like a python and chomping him to bits.

He jumped as a knock sounded at the door.

"Boys, I asked you to stop knocking," said Dad from his room.

Derek looked at Sam.

"It wasn't me..." said Sam.

The knock sounded again. It was coming from the door to the hallway.

"Maybe it's the alligator," laughed Derek.

"Room service," a familiar voice called through the door.

"We didn't order anything," shouted Derek from the bed.

"I have a large selection of candy bars," the voice answered back.

Sam walked over to the door and stood on his tiptoes to see through the peephole. Caitlin's face was on the other side, distorted into a weird shape from the glass in the peephole, like in a house of mirrors at an amusement park.

Sam opened the door. "Well, maybe just this once."

Caitlin smiled and walked into the room. "Thank you very much, sir."

"Hey, where's our candy bars?" asked Derek.

"Oh, silly me!" said Caitlin, patting her pockets. "I must have left them downstairs. Sorry about that!"

Sam's dad walked into the room through the center doorway. "Oh, hi Caitlin. Where did you come from?"

"Hi, Mr. Jackson. Your wife asked me to tell you that Robert would like you to join them across the street for drinks."

"She did, did she?" said Dad, fighting back a yawn.

"I thought everyone was going to bed?" said Derek.

"Apparently, Anita's too worked up to sleep," explained Caitlin.

Derek patted Dad on the back, stepping forward to the doorway with a grin. "Why don't you stay here and rest, Dad. I'll go have drinks with Mr. Wonder   I mean, Robert."

Dad shook his head. "Nice try. I think I'll be okay."

"You're not staying over at the hotel tonight, are you?" Sam asked Caitlin.

Caitlin shook her head. "No, we're leaving in a few minutes. Daddy's double checking the lights for the wedding tomorrow. He wants everything to be perfect. He says that Robert is a very demanding client with high expectations."

Derek laughed. "That sounds about right."

"I just wanted to say goodbye." Caitlin reached out and gave Sam a hug. "Be careful tonight." He did his best not to pull away. For some reason, Caitlin liked to give him hugs. Maybe she'd stop if she realized the grief that Derek gave him about it.

"Okay," said Sam, finally breaking free. "We will. Don't worry. See you."

"Bye, Derek," Caitlin called as she turned and walked to the door.

"What, no hug for me?" Derek scoffed.

Caitlin rolled her eyes and gave a faint wave.

Dad walked back into the room with his phone and wallet in his hands. "I'll walk you down to the lobby, Caitlin." He stopped short of the door. "Can I count on you two to behave and go to bed soon?"

"Okay," said Sam.

"Absolutely," said Derek, faking a yawn. "I'm so tired."

Dad lowered his eyes and gave Derek a serious look.

"What?" said Derek. "Yes, we'll go to bed." Dad shook his head and pulled the door shut behind him.

Derek sat down on one of the double beds in their room. He fooled with the TV remote until he found a West Coast NBA game on ESPN. Sam changed into his pajamas and then went into the bathroom and brushed his teeth. He was pretty sleepy. It had been a busy day. He thought about the alligator and shivered. He could still feel those beady eyes staring at him.

He used the toilet and walked back out into the bedroom. The basketball game was playing on the TV, but Derek wasn't there.

"Derek?"

Derek was probably hiding somewhere to scare him. Sam walked around to the other side of the bed, but it was empty. He opened the adjoining door and looked into Mom and Dad's room. Everything was dark.

"I know you're in here, Derek."

He fumbled along the wall, bracing himself at each step for Derek to jump out. His knee banged against something hard. "Ouch!" His finger finally found the light switch and flicked it on. This room was empty too. What the heck?

Where could Derek have gone? He was there just a minute ago. Did he go down to the lobby? Why wouldn't he have told Sam before he left? Didn't he care that there was a wild alligator roaming around?

Sam went back to his room. He opened the door, sticking his head out. The hall was silent, except for a low hum and a crunching sound around the corner to his right.

"Derek?"

He quietly stepped into the hall in his bare feet. The crunching sound grew louder with each step down the hallway. Sam slowed, his mind filling with images of alligators.

"Derek?" he whispered again, but there was no answer.

Just the sound.

Crunch, crunch, hum.

CHAPTER THIRTEEN

S am reached the corner of the hall. The crunch, crunch, hum sound seemed to be just on the other side of the wall. Maybe it was the alligator meticulously chomping Derek to pieces.

Sam tried to be brave. It couldn't be an alligator...could it?

Slowly he slipped his head past the edge of the wall, eyes wide with expectation. All at once, he leaped into the opening. "Kiai!" Sam screamed with a dramatic karate chop.

The small side room was empty. No alligators with sharp teeth. No Derek. Just a tall, brown machine with the word *ICE* written on it. Crunch, crunch, hum, it ran, as ice cubes fell inside it.

Sam smacked his forehead with his hand. He felt stupid. Again. He glanced around casually to make sure no one had seen him.

"Well where the heck did he go then?" Sam said out loud. He turned back down the hallway to his room. It was just like Derek to run off and leave him alone in the room with no warning and a wild alligator on the loose.

Sam turned the door handle to his room and pushed. It didn't budge. He pushed harder. It must have locked by itself. He patted down the pockets of his flannel pajamas, but he didn't have the key card to his room. "That's just great."

He couldn't just stand there in the hall waiting for Derek. Someone else might come along. Or some*thing*. He ran toward the elevator, then stopped short. What if something was already in it when the doors opened? He didn't want to get trapped. He wasn't that high up. He would take the stairs.

Sam gripped the railing tightly as he inched down the marble steps in the side stairwell that led toward the lobby. He felt ridiculous in his bare feet and pajamas and was glad that Caitlin had already gone home so she wouldn't see him. The balcony of the Rotunda was at the bottom of the flight of stairs. He kept his eyes peeled for Mom or Dad. Derek had to be around here somewhere too. Maybe Mo could help him, although Sam really didn't trust him.

He looked around the balcony. The only people watching him were the former American presidents that lined the walls in stately old paintings. As he tiptoed across the carpet, a voice called out softly.

"Nice pajamas."

Sam spun around in the direction of the sound. Derek was crouched against the side of the balcony behind a large potted palm tree. Sam sighed loudly and walked over to his brother, who was staring down into the Rotunda.

"What are you doing down here?"

"Shh," whispered Derek from his position behind the plant. "Get down."

Sam gritted his teeth and tried to have patience. He knelt down next to Derek. "What are you doing?" he repeated.

"I'm staking out the lobby," said Derek.

"Staking it out for who?" He looked over the railing but didn't see anyone. The hotel seemed to have mostly gone to bed.

"Not who," said Derek, pointing toward the staircase. "What."

Sam shook his head. "*What* are you talking about?" He leaned forward to get a better view. "I don't see anything."

"The alligator," said Derek, motioning again toward the stairs. "It's down there. It keeps walking around the staircase."

Sam's eyes lit up. "What?" He stood up quickly. "We need to tell somebody."

Derek shook his head.

"What do you mean, no? Are you crazy?"

"No," answered Derek. "It vanished."

"Vanished? Like disappeared?"

Derek grinned. "Vanished like under the wall."

"What wall?"

Derek pointed to the spot near the stairs where they'd been looking before the rehearsal dinner. "It must have found a way down into the tunnels like Mo was saying." He stood up and headed down the staircase.

"Where are you going?" asked Sam.

"To check it out. Where else?"

Sam's heart raced. "Wait!" He tugged at Derek's shirt. "What if it gets us? We'd be trapped. We should call Mo."

Derek paused, crouching down. "Hmm. For once, Sam, you're actually right. We *should* call Mo." He looked around the balcony, then snapped his fingers. "I've got it."

"Got what?"

"Stay here." Derek casually walked over to an antique black phone on a table against the wall. He put the large receiver up to his ear and pushed a button.

He began talking in a deep voice. "Yes, I need a bellman to help me with my bags...can you send that nice man, Mo Peterson, up to my room?" He paused to listen to the person on the other end of the line. "Yes, Room 515. Thank you."

Derek walked back over to Sam with a big smile on his face. "That should keep him busy for a little while."

"But our room isn't 515..." said Sam.

"Exactly. It's on the other side of the hotel. It will

77

take Mo a long time to get there and back, so we have time to check out the passageway."

Sam shook his head. "What? We need his help, not to send him away!"

"He'll never let us go down there. We need time to find the passageway. Besides, they already think you're the one who opened the cage."

Sam frowned at his brother. "They do not! You know I didn't do it."

Derek grinned. "I know it, but I'm not the one who can put you in the slammer." He ran down the staircase, staying close to the side to keep out of view.

"This is ridiculous," groaned Sam, a bead of sweat gathering on his forehead.

Sam watched Derek move his hands carefully over the section of the wall next to the stairs. He knocked on it lightly like their dad did when he was trying to find a wall joist. Sam turned away from Derek to look up at the entrance to the Palm Court. There was no sign of Mom and Dad. The place seemed to be deserted.

He looked back at the wall, but Derek wasn't there. He was gone. He'd vanished.

CHAPTER FOURTEEN

S am hustled over to where Derek had been, next to the grand staircase.

"Derek!" he said in barely a whisper. He looked at the wall for some kind of opening. "He did it again..." Sam muttered.

He moved forward, feeling with his fingers for some kind of crack. The wall seemed rock solid. His bare feet felt cold on the tile floor. Really cold.

He bent down and felt along the bottom of the wall. A cool breeze was flowing out from a gap between the wall and the floor. It was like there was an empty space behind it. He noticed two small squares, indented into the wall. They were even with his shoulders, about a foot across from each other. Sam put a hand on each square and pushed. All at once, a section of the wall sprung open like a narrow door. Sam stared into the dark space under the staircase. He caught his breath as the cool air poured out over him. He felt chill bumps down his arms. "This is it."

Sam glanced over his shoulder into the Rotunda. He couldn't imagine a good reason to go in the passage, but he knew he would. He always seemed to follow his older brother, even when it ended up getting him in trouble. Which was most of the time.

Before he could think about it any longer, a radio squawked from around the corner. It was Mo! Now he didn't have a choice. Sam leaped into the opening and pushed the doorway closed. He stood frozen inside the wall, listening, as Mo's footsteps walked past him. He must not have seen.

Sam turned around inside the wall and realized that he couldn't see anything either. It was pitch black.

"Derek?" he whispered, pressing his hands against the closest wall. He didn't want to think about what could be in the dark with him, but he couldn't help it. From what Mo had said, it had been a hundred years since they rebuilt the hotel after the fire. Had anyone else been down here since then?

He calmed himself by remembering that Derek had to be nearby. He'd only entered the passageway a few minutes before. How far could he have gone? Unless the alligator already had him.

Sam pushed such thoughts out of his mind and moved forward. His foot slipped over a step leading down and he nearly fell. The concrete was hard underneath his feet. He gathered his balance and slowly descended a staircase.

"Derek!" he whispered again in the darkness. He reached the bottom of the stairs without hearing a reply. He groped along the wall, looking for a light switch. Suddenly his fingers landed on something soft. Fleshy. Like a body. Sam's heart leapt.

"Took you long enough," said Derek, through the darkness, pushing Sam's hand away from his arm.

Sam let out a long breath. "What are you doing? You nearly scared me to death."

"I'm channeling my inner gator, letting my eyes adjust to the darkness. You can see pretty well after a while."

"What is this place?" Sam asked, the darkness gradually turning into shadows. He could now make out a long hallway, but it only seemed to end in more darkness. A very faint glow came from dim lights spaced every so often near the ceiling. They were so old and covered with dirt that the light hardly shined through.

"I don't know," said Derek. "It must be one of those passages under the city that connects all the buildings."

"So what are we going to do now that we're down here?" asked Sam.

Derek crouched down. "Check this out." The cement floor was covered with a thick layer of dust and dirt. That wasn't surprising after being hidden away for a hundred years.

"What is it?"

"Tracks," said Derek.

Sam bent down. Sure enough, there were marks in the dirt. They looked like scrapes. Or claws. Like something was being dragged along the floor. He gulped, picturing an alligator dragging him along.

Sam hopped up. "Okay. Time to go."

"What? We just got here. We have to follow them."

Sam shook his head. "No way. That's enough for me. I'm out of here."

Derek put his hand on Sam's arm. "Shh."

"Quit it. You already scared me once."

"No, seriously." Derek held still and listened. "I heard something."

Sam strained to listen through the darkness. He didn't *want* to hear anything, but he did. A noise was coming from the top of the stairs where they'd entered the wall. Someone, or something, was coming from the hotel!

"Come on, we have to hide," said Derek.

They scrambled down the hall until they came to a metal door on one side. Derek pointed to a small sign mounted on the wall beside the doorframe. He brushed at the dust with his hand.

Sam gasped. "*L. Ginter.*"

Derek put his finger up to his lips.

Lewis Ginter? Why would he have had a secret room built this far below the hotel? The footsteps coming down the stairs were growing closer. They needed to get into this room, whatever it was.

Derek carefully turned the doorknob. Surprisingly, it opened. Without knowing exactly what they were walking in to, they slid into the room. The door let out a loud creak as it closed behind them. Surely anyone coming down the stairs would have heard that. Sam scooted against the wall until he found something that felt sturdy enough to hide behind. Derek pushed himself up against the wall behind where the door would open.

Sam held his breath. Listening. Someone was walking toward them. The footsteps stopped right outside the door. He heard the handle turn.

The door slowly opened.

CHAPTER FIFTEEN

A figure stood in the doorway. It seemed short, like a kid. A hand reached up to the wall, feeling for a light switch. Suddenly the room was filled with brightness.

"It's you!" Derek exclaimed.

Sam's eyes opened wide as he peered up from behind an old desk. "Nathan? What are you doing down here?"

Nathan looked down at Sam on the floor. "I could ask you the same thing."

"We're following the alligator," said Derek. "We think it came down the passageway in the wall."

"And I'm following you," said Nathan, a smirk on his face. "I was watching you two bumble around in the Rotunda." He folded his arms and frowned at Sam. "I'm keeping my eye on you so I can prove what you did."

Sam shook his head. "Give me a break." He crawled out from under the desk and looked around the small room. It was about half the size of his bedroom at home. It looked like an old supply room that had been converted into an office. Or maybe it was an old office that had been converted into a supply room. It was hard to tell. Whatever it was, it didn't look like anyone had been in there for years.

The metal desk he'd hidden under was pushed against one wall next to a small bookshelf. A green cot on the other side of the room looked like it might collapse if he sat on it. It had more holes than fabric. There were piles of rolled-up paper, like the kind architects use for building plans or maps, on every surface. The whole place had a very lived-in – but deserted – feel. Who would want to be down here? It didn't look like a very nice place to stay.

"Do you think this room was really Lewis Ginter's, like it said on the sign by the door?" asked Sam.

"What's that?" asked Nathan, pointing to a large map on the wall above the desk. It looked like the whole world. The old paper had an assortment of red lines drawn back and forth, most of them across the oceans.

"Who knows," replied Derek. "Maybe it's a map of where he bought his alligators."

Sam stared closer. There was writing on top of each red line. *June 14, 1888.*

He followed that line with his finger. It started in Richmond, went to Chicago, then San Francisco, then across the ocean to Hawaii, then to Australia. Sam leaned back. There were lines like that all over the map. There had to be at least thirty of them, all across the world. "Wow…he was an explorer."

Derek stepped up next to Sam and looked at the map. "Or maybe an adventurer. Like us!" He smiled.

Sam tried to think about crossing the ocean thirty times. It must have been by boat back then, too. He shook his head. He didn't really want to go anywhere in a boat, let alone across the ocean. He felt seasick just thinking about it. Sam stepped away from the map and frowned. "We need to get out of here and go back to the hotel. We're never going to find anything."

"How 'bout my game? Did you find *that* yet?" asked Nathan, staring accusingly at Sam across the room.

"Nathan, I didn't take it," said Sam.

"I thought you were going to check the zoo?" said Derek, smiling.

"The loo," barked Nathan. "And I did. It wasn't there."

"Maybe you dropped it in," said Derek.

Nathan shook his head.

"Did you ask Mo?" said Sam, walking back to the doorway. He peered out into the darkness.

"No, not yet," said Nathan.

"We think maybe he stole the wedding rings," said Derek.

"What's this thing?" Nathan said, picking up an object made of metal and glass from the bookshelf.

"It's a lantern, I think," said Sam. It reminded him of the one that their dad brought along when they went camping. They usually hung that one from a tree while they sat around the campfire. This one looked a lot older though.

Derek wiped dust off a section of the glass. "I think you're right. It looks like it runs on oil." He unscrewed a small round cover. "See? Here's the tank on the bottom."

"Oil?" asked Nathan. "Like the black stuff in the tanker ships?"

Derek shook his head. "No, lantern oil. It's more like gasoline."

Nathan scrunched his eyebrows together. "Oh, you mean petrol."

"Uh...no," answered Derek. "I mean gas. Like for your car. You do have cars in England, don't you?"

"Shove off," muttered Nathan. "Yes, we have cars. We call gas *petrol*."

Sam shook his head. These English words were so strange.

"Now if we are lucky..." Derek began searching through the desk drawers. "Aha!" He pulled out a dirty box of matches.

"Those will never work," said Nathan.

"Dude, have a little faith," Derek replied, opening the top of the lantern. He pulled out a match from the box and struck it quickly against the desk.

Nothing happened.

"Told you," said Nathan.

Derek nodded and pulled out another match, flicking it on his pants this time. Still nothing happened.

"He's probably right," said Sam. "They've been down here a long time, maybe they got wet."

Derek's face grew more determined. He pulled out a third match and struck it against the concrete wall. Instantly, a spark burst into flame at the end of the matchstick. He quickly lowered the match into the top of the glass panel, holding it still to light the wick.

"Ouch!" He jerked his hand back from the flame, dropping the match and shaking his fingers. He bent down to watch the wick slowly begin to burn, turning the knob on the base of the lantern until the flame was steady.

Derek looked at Nathan, raising his eyebrows in delight. "You were saying?" He lifted the lantern by a wire handle and walked to the doorway. "You ladies can stay here and argue about video games if you want. I'm following the gator tracks."

Sam sighed and stepped toward the doorway.

"I thought you were scared," said Nathan.

"I am," said Sam, nodding. "But I'm not staying here with you!"

They followed the tracks in the dirt further down the hallway. The lantern light was not overly bright, but it was much better than nothing. Derek moved in a slight crouch, holding the lantern close to the ground so he could see the tracks. Sam felt his bare feet growing dirty from the floor. He wished he had his shoes. And that he wasn't in his pajamas. And that they weren't chasing an alligator.

They followed the tracks around several bends and turns in the passageway. Sam looked behind them. Would they even be able to find their way back? "I think this is far enough."

Derek paused and stood up straight. He held his hand up in a *stop* motion, not making a sound. Sam peered ahead of them into the shadows. What was it?

Derek picked up a loose piece of stone and tossed it up ahead of them. A dark shadow scurried away from the wall and around a corner, out of sight. Sam's heart froze.

"Did you see that?" hissed Nathan.

Derek hustled forward with the lantern, leading them toward the movement. They came to a ragged opening in the stone wall. The opening was supported by two wooden beams, placed at an angle against the stone. Sam couldn't tell if it was a doorframe that was falling down, or a hole in the wall that had been supported to make a doorway. It reminded him of pictures of old crumbling buildings that were about to be knocked down. Sam stared up at the beams in the shadows. They looked rickety.

Derek held the lantern through the opening. It was another room. A shadow moved along the back wall.

"What was that?" asked Sam, his legs starting to tremble. "Was it...an alligator?"

"I don't know," said Derek. "Come on."

"What?" gasped Sam. "No way, I'm staying here."

Derek stepped forward with the lantern. "Fine. Stay

there." He moved toward the shadow, with Nathan following behind.

"Derek!" Sam shouted in frustration. He glanced around at the darkness. "Wait!" he whispered, running to catch up.

They walked through another tunnel. This one felt more like they were underground than in a planned hallway. There were spots in the ceiling where water dripped, leaving small streams along the wall and the floor. It was hard to tell in the near darkness, but it felt like they were going down. As if the earth was swallowing them up.

They came to a turn and Derek stopped. The air was cool and filled with the distant sound of running water. Sam thought of the *crunch crunch hum* sound up in the hotel. He'd thought he was scared then… this was much worse.

Derek crouched down and studied the dirt again under the lantern light. "Something's in there," he whispered.

"How do you know?" asked Nathan, hesitation filling his voice.

"I can sense it," answered Derek.

Sam groaned, then did something surprising.

Maybe he was sick of Derek always telling him what to do. Maybe it was because his feet hurt. Maybe he was tired of always getting scared for no reason.

"This is stupid," he yelled, grabbing the lantern. He pushed past Derek and Nathan. "There's nothing out there. It's just the shadows playing tricks on us. You probably didn't even see the alligator come down here. We need to get the heck out of here before we get lost." He stepped around the corner.

"See!" he proclaimed, holding the lantern up high in front of him. Light streamed into an enormous, open room. It seemed to stretch on forever, like some hidden underground cavern. Water dripped from open cracks above them. Pillars of rock hung down from the ceiling.

Derek's mouth dropped open. "Oh my gosh..."

Sam's arm turned to stone, the lantern dangling from his hand like a light post. He couldn't move a muscle, except for his eyes, which darted around the deep room of shadows. A wide pool of water lay in the middle of the space as if it had been filled by a hundred years of rainwater working its way underground.

Lying all around the pool were alligators.

Dozens of them.

CHAPTER SIXTEEN

"Sam," whispered Derek, "don't move."

Nathan didn't say anything, he just stared.

Sam tried to find his voice, but his mouth was bone dry. He blinked his eyes, hoping he was dreaming. The beady, red eyes of the gators reflected in the lantern light. He could hear their breathing echoing off the rock walls in a low hum. One of the closest ones began to inch toward the doorway. Its nails scraped along the rocks as it moved.

"Derek..." Sam managed to say in barely a whisper.

The alligator started moving faster. Its mouth opened, showing rows of yellow teeth like knives. It was coming right at him.

Nathan whimpered, turning to take off back down the hallway.

"Run!" cried Derek, pulling on Sam's shirt.

But Sam couldn't move. His bare feet felt like they were glued to the dirty floor.

"Sam, run!" Derek yelled again, pulling him backward. As Sam tumbled into the hall, the lantern slipped from his grasp. Glass shattered and the small oil tank exploded into a fireball.

Sam and Derek lay frozen on the ground, watching the flames and shadows dance around the room in an eerie glow. The closest alligator snapped his head away from the fire. Behind him, long bodies dove into the dark pool of water.

"Let's get out of here!" Derek cried.

They scrambled off the ground and followed Nathan down the hall.

"Which way is the hotel?" asked Derek.

"I don't know," Nathan panted. "There are so many hallways."

This was what Sam had been afraid of. They were going to be lost underground forever. He looked back over his shoulder, the glow of the flames brightening the tunnel. He saw a shadow against the wall growing larger. The alligator was coming after them!

"Oomph," Sam moaned, slamming into something solid. He bounced off, landing on his back. He stared up at the wooden beam in the crumbling opening they'd come to. He'd been so focused on watching behind him that he'd run smack into it.

"Look out!" shouted Nathan, just as Sam noticed the wood begin to slide sideways. Sam scurried to his feet and through the opening as an avalanche of rocks began to tumble toward the ground.

Derek tugged Sam's arm again. "Let's go!" he shouted, as he raced down the hall. This time, Sam didn't turn around to see if they were being followed. He just ran.

"Which way?" called Nathan, when they came to a crossing in the tunnels. "I don't remember how we came."

Derek looked back and forth. "I'm not sure…but let's try this one." He turned down the left tunnel.

"How do you know?" said Sam.

"I don't," replied Derek, as they ran. "But any way is better than back there."

They continued down the tunnel until they came to a door in the wall. Nathan pulled on the handle. "It's stuck!"

"Here, let me try," said Derek, pushing Nathan out of the way. He shifted all his weight and knocked into the door like a linebacker making a big hit. The door flung open. They hustled through, pushing the door shut behind them, the noise of it echoing through the tunnel.

Without the lantern, this new space was even darker than the passageway. Sam couldn't see a thing. They all fumbled again along the walls, but there was no switch. Sam's head banged against a metal pole. "Ouch!"

"I think we're in a stairwell," said Derek. He patted something in the darkness that made an iron clang. "It's like in a lighthouse. The steps spiral upward."

Sam's stomach turned. He hated lighthouses. They made him dizzy. One time, they had climbed one at the beach, and Dad had almost had to carry him down, he was so scared.

Sam looked up and tried to see in the darkness. There seemed to be some light higher up, but not much. "Where do they go?"

"Up," said Derek, moving past him. "Come on."

Sam carefully felt his way one step at a time up the curve of the stairs. After a bit, he started to feel more confident. He tried to relax his death grip on the railing. "Where are we going?" he panted, already winded.

"Anywhere but down there," said Nathan. "Unless you want to be stuck in that flaming lake of alligators."

Sam kept climbing. For once, he agreed with Nathan. But he couldn't help getting discouraged. How many steps were there? It felt like they'd been climbing forever. He kept looking over his shoulder, imagining that he heard something crawling after them.

Finally, they reached a small landing. It was wide enough for the three boys to squeeze onto next to each other. They tried to catch their breath.

"Where are we?" asked Sam.

"I don't know," answered Derek.

"Do you think alligators can climb stairs?" asked Nathan.

"No," said Derek. "I think we're safe."

Sam wasn't so sure. He might have agreed with Derek before this, but not after seeing a lake of alligators below the hotel. Who knows what else could happen?

They started climbing again, and after a minute, they reached the end of the stairs. There was no door, just a narrow opening in the stone wall.

"Come on," called Derek, crawling in.

Sam shook his head as Nathan began to follow Derek into the hole. "I'm not going in there."

"It's okay," called Derek. "I'm through."

Sam swallowed hard and crawled on his knees. He certainly couldn't stay at the top of the metal stairway alone. He inched along, trying not to think of what might be in the tunnel with him. After a few feet, he bumped into Nathan's shoe as he stopped to exit.

"Told you," said Derek.

Sam ignored him and stood up, looking around. He saw more stairs, but these were different, looking more like the side stairs that led to the guestroom hallways in the hotel.

"Do you think we're above ground now?" asked Nathan. "In The Jefferson?"

Derek pointed to some light above them in the stairway. "We have to be. That's moonlight. Or city light. One or the other."

Sam stepped toward a door next to them.

"It's locked," said Derek. "I already tried."

Nathan groaned, pushing past them to the next staircase. "Let's see if there's a way out up here."

When they reached the next landing, its door was

locked too. So was the next one. And the one after that. It was hopeless.

"What do we do now?" said Sam. They were at the top. There were no more stairs, just a metal ladder on the wall that led up to the ceiling.

Derek shrugged and stepped over to a big window that was on the side of the top landing. He pressed his nose against the glass, looking up at the night sky. "I think we're in a bell tower." He turned back toward them. "Remember when we drove in, there were two clock towers?"

Sam nodded. They'd looked kind of like church steeple towers but without the steeples.

Nathan placed a foot on the crusty ladder rung and started up. "Then this must lead to the bells. There's no way an alligator can follow us up a ladder."

Sam shook his head. "We don't need to go up. We need to get out." He stared up into the shadows of the ceiling, following the crusty metal bars with his eyes until they vanished somewhere in the roof. "Where does it even go?"

Nathan ignored him and kept climbing. Derek put a foot on the ladder and started up behind him.

"Where are you going?" Sam hissed.

"We might as well follow him," Derek answered.

Sam shook his head. "Just great." He looked up. Nathan was almost to the top.

Something hard hit Sam on the head. "Ouch!" he

yelled. Whatever had hit him clanged down on the cement floor. It made a distinct metallic sound.

"What was that?" called Derek from halfway up the ladder.

"I don't know," said Sam, rubbing his forehead. "Something bonked me on the head." He crouched down and felt around on the floor with his hands, trying to find what had hit him. He touched something hard and round.

Maybe it was a coin. He remembered the Indian Head penny that Derek had once found in a cave. This could be another rare coin. The building was definitely old enough. But as he picked it up, his fingers curled around the narrow edges. It wasn't a coin.

It was a ring.

CHAPTER SEVENTEEN

S am held the ring up toward Nathan in the ceiling. It looked like he and Derek had found some kind of trap door that led to the bell tower. Before Sam could call out, a loud bang echoed from below. Something was coming.

Sam's heart raced. What was it? Had one of the alligators broken through the door? Maybe it was Mo.

He couldn't think straight, but he knew he had to act fast. He stuck his foot on the rusty ladder and began scaling the wall. He didn't dare look down. He knew that if he slipped he'd plummet to the concrete landing and, likely, his death. He just kept climbing, trying to block out the sound below him.

"Come on," whispered Derek from the space above.

Sam swallowed hard and reached up. The metal bars on the ladder hurt his bare feet. He started to feel dizzy.

Was the bell tower spinning? He began swaying backward, like a magnet was pulling at him from the ground below. He was going to fall!

Suddenly, Derek's hands grabbed his arm, pulling him back to safety.

"Oh my gosh!" cried Sam, breathing hard on the floor of the bell tower. Sweat beaded on his forehead.

Nathan was sitting by the wall, shaking his head. "Classic," he muttered.

Sam remembered why he'd come up. "Quick, shut the door! Quietly…something's coming!" Derek lowered the wooden door back over the opening.

Sam leaned forward, peering around the new room. It was cold and dark. A mixture of moonlight and light from the city created a hazy glow all around them. A chilly breeze blew in from the windows all around the tower. There was no glass, just wide-open spaces to let out the sound from the bells. He shivered, his pajamas too thin to protect him from the cold.

Sam felt the ring in his pocket. He pulled it out, holding it in front of Nathan's face. "Know anything about this?"

"What is it?" asked Derek, looking closer. "A ring?" He tilted his head. "Where did you get a ring up here?"

"It fell on my head."

"It fell on your—oh!" Derek's face brightened. They both stared at Nathan.

"It feels like a wedding ring," said Sam. "Know anyone missing one of those, Nathan?"

Nathan sat silently in the shadows.

"Well?" asked Derek.

A faint sound came from Nathan's side of the room. At first, Sam thought it was a mouse squeaking. When he realized what it was, he tried to soften his voice. "Are you crying?"

Nathan gave a big sniff. "No."

"Yes you are," said Derek. "*You* stole the rings, didn't you?"

"Why?" asked Sam.

Nathan let out a long breath. "I don't want this bloody wedding, that's why."

"Why not?" asked Sam.

"Because things were fine the way they were! My dad and me. Ever since Mum died, it's just been us. Together. It was fine." He sniffed again. "Then he had to go and fancy Anita and decide to move to America."

"What's wrong with America?" asked Derek.

"Yeah," said Sam. "And Anita seems nice, isn't she?"

"Oh, sure, she's lovely," said Nathan. "But I don't want to move again. I don't know anyone here. I liked it how we were."

"That does sound hard," said Sam. "You know, when Derek and I moved to Virginia from up North a few years ago, we didn't know anyone either."

"At least you had each other," said Nathan.

"Yeah, but it's *Sam...*" said Derek.

Sam ignored him. "True, we did have each other, but it was still hard to be in a new place."

"Then we started having adventures," said Derek.

"And we met new friends, too," said Sam. "It worked out okay." He reached over and handed Nathan the ring. "Here. I think you should give it back. Your dad really does seem to love her. Taking the rings isn't going to stop the wedding."

Nathan took the ring from Sam's hand. "I guess you're right."

"But setting a wild alligator loose to roam free in the hotel," said Derek, "that was a much better move. Pretty stupid, but effective."

"What do you mean?" asked Nathan.

"Oh, please," said Derek. "You don't have to pretend. You let it out, didn't you? To stop the wedding."

Nathan scooted closer to them. "No, honest, I didn't do that. I don't know how it got loose."

Derek shook his head like he wasn't convinced. "I think that if you stole the rings, you probably set the alligator loose too. And then you blamed all of it on poor Sam." He patted Sam on the back.

Sam nodded in wary agreement. He always got suspicious when Derek spoke up for him.

"Now, ordinarily," Derek continued, "I'd be all for sticking something bad on Sam, but this has gone a bit too far. Even for me."

"I told you. I didn't do it!" exclaimed Nathan, standing up. "Why don't you just shove off." He pushed away from them, as if to head back down the ladder. His foot caught on a board sticking up in the floor, throwing himself off balance. He went sprawling onto the floor, the ring flying from his hand and across the room. It bounced once on the brick window ledge, and then was sucked up into the night.

CHAPTER EIGHTEEN

"No!" Nathan shrieked. He lunged for the window and the ring, but he was too late. He stared blankly into the darkness, shaking his head.

Derek came over and carefully leaned out the window. "Wait, there it is, sitting on the ledge!"

Sam peered over Derek's shoulder. Sure enough, the ring had landed on a ledge, several feet away from the window. It glimmered in the city lights on the cold, dark ledge of the bell tower.

"What are you doing?" asked Derek.

Sam turned back to see Nathan with one leg already through the window opening. He was stepping out onto the ledge. Was he crazy? "Nathan, get back in here! It's too dangerous."

"I have to get it," said Nathan, shaking his head. "I have to make things right."

Sam leaned his head as far out the window as he

dared. He looked down to the parking lot and the street below. It was way too high. He moved back into the room and leaned against the wall, feeling dizzy.

"I think I can reach it," said Nathan, grunting as he kneeled down, his hand stretched out. He inched toward the ring, his other hand pressed up against the bell tower for balance. "Almost got it…"

Sam watched from the next window. Nathan's fingers brushed the ring, nudging it away from him. "Almost…" he groaned, just before his leg slipped on a patch of ice. "Whoa!" he screamed, his momentum nearly carrying him over the edge. The ring slipped over the side into the darkness below.

"Nathan!" Sam and Derek yelled in unison.

Nathan reached out and grabbed one of the brick ledges, pulling himself back toward the building.

"Oh my gosh!" said Sam, shaking hard even though he wasn't the one on the ledge.

"Get back in here, Nathan. You're going to get your-self killed," Derek exclaimed.

Nathan stood frozen, his back pressed against the bricks. "I dropped the ring!" he sobbed. "My dad is going to kill me."

"It's okay," called Sam. "He'll be a lot more upset if you fall off that ledge. Come back in."

Nathan carefully shook his head. "I can't….m-m-move," he stuttered.

Sam looked at his brother. "What should we do? We can't just leave him."

"Well I'm not going out there," said Derek. "Why don't you get him?"

"I can't," said Sam, staring out the window. "It's too high."

"Then what?"

Sam tried to think. Maybe they could throw him something to hold. He looked around the dark room. A rope hung from the ceiling, but it was too short. It would never reach out the window. "We need someone to help us."

"That's it!" Derek reached up and touched the rope hanging from the ceiling. "I have an idea."

Sam shook his head. "I already thought of that. It's too short. It won't reach him."

Derek grinned. "Nathan's not who I'm trying to reach." He held onto the rope with both hands, like he was going to climb it, then he tugged with all his weight.

Clang! An enormous sound rang out. Of course. The bells!

"Ahh!" screamed Nathan. "What was that?"

"Chillax," muttered Derek. "It's your rescue."

Sam leaned out the window. He hadn't thought about Nathan being startled by the sound. Maybe they should have warned him. "Hold on! We're calling for help."

"Help?" cried Nathan. "You're going to make me fall!"

Sam covered his ears as Derek rang the bells again. It

did seem like the whole bell tower might crumble down around them.

"That should get someone's attention," said Derek, releasing the rope after a bunch of rings.

The boys talked to Nathan, trying to keep him calm, until the sound of a door banged from below.

"Hello? Is somebody up there?" a voice called. It was Mo.

Sam didn't really care who it was at this point. They just needed help.

"Up here!" shouted Derek. "In the bell tower." He bent over and pulled back the trap door.

"Who's up there?" said Mo.

Sam peered through the opening, careful not to crawl too close to the edge. "It's us. Sam and Derek and Nathan."

"What on earth are you doin' up there, boys? Hang tight, I'm coming up."

Soon, Mo's face came into view at the top of the ladder.

"Nathan's stuck out on the ledge," said Sam. "You have to save him!"

CHAPTER NINETEEN

Mo hustled over to the window, leaning out to see Nathan, still pressed against the wall. "Hold on, son. I'm coming." He turned to Derek. "Hold my belt."

Derek grabbed the back of Mo's belt as Mo held onto the window frame with one hand, and reached for Nathan with the other. "It's okay, son. Just reach out for my hand. Nice and slow-like."

Sam moved back to the other window so he could see. "It's okay, Nathan. Take Mo's hand."

"I can't," said Nathan. "I'm stuck. My feet won't move."

"Yes, you can, Nathan," said Mo. "Just take one step at a time."

Nathan stood still for a moment. Then barely, almost unnoticeably, he took a tiny step toward Mo. He eased his arm out toward Mo's, keeping his back pressed against the wall. As soon as he came within reach, Mo snatched Nathan's wrist. "Gotcha!"

In one quick motion, Mo reeled Nathan inside the window. Nathan was shivering. It must have been even colder out on the ledge than it was in the bell tower.

Mo pulled a handkerchief from his back pocket and wiped his forehead. "Oh, me," he said, sitting down against the wall. "You boys are puttin' me through my paces today." He looked across at them. "What are you doing up here, anyway? This isn't a good place for kids."

"Well..." Sam didn't know where to begin.

"We followed the alligator into the passageway under the stairs," explained Derek.

Mo turned his head crooked. "What's that now?"

Sam nodded. "And we found Lewis Ginter's secret office."

Mo raised his eyebrows.

"But then we found Alligator Lake and Sam threw a firebomb at it," said Derek, smiling. "It was great."

Mo's eyes opened wide. "Alligator Lake?"

"So we ran away into the stairwell," said Sam. "We kept climbing until we reached the top. We thought they were coming after us."

"Who was?" asked Mo.

"The alligators!" exclaimed Sam. "Lots of them."

"But then I lost the ring," moaned Nathan, putting his hand over his face.

"The ring?" asked Mo. "Did you find them?"

"Um..." said Nathan. "I kind of took them."

"*You* took them!" shouted Mo. "Why in tarnation would you do that? We've been looking all over for those rings."

"I know," said Nathan. "I'm sorry. I'm going to give them back. If I ever find the other one." He peered out the window to the ground below. "I didn't think I was going to make it back when I was out there on the ledge. I realized that things could actually be a lot worse. I guess it won't be that bad having to move here with Dad and Anita."

Mo whistled. "Quite a conundrum you've gotten yourself into, son."

Sam turned his head. "Conundrum?" He'd never heard that word before. If Caitlin were here she'd explain it to him.

Mo chuckled. "It's a difficult problem."

Nathan sighed. "That's for sure."

Mo looked back down at them. "How did you boys say you got down in the sub-basement?"

"We found the secret door under the grand staircase," said Sam. "Just like you said."

"Ha!" Mo cackled. "I did, did I?" He scratched his head. "I'm not sure that I even believed that one."

"Actually, I found the door," said Derek. "You just followed me."

"Whatever," said Sam.

Mo put his hand on Nathan's shoulder. "Oh, and by the way, son. I found your video game."

"You did?" said Nathan, his eyes growing wide.

"Uh, huh. It was in the restroom wastebasket. Must've been knocked off the counter."

Sam narrowed his eyes toward Nathan. "See! I told you I didn't steal it."

Nathan shook his head. "I'm sorry." He looked like he was about to start crying again. "I've just messed everything up."

"Well, it's at the front desk. You can pick it up when we get out of here," said Mo.

"Wait a minute," said Derek. "What about the alligators? Are you just going to leave them down there?"

Mo raised his eyebrows. "You boys have quite the imaginations. I'm not sure I follow you. We found the missing alligator a little while ago. It was hiding back in the bellman's closet."

"Wait..." said Sam. "You found the missing alligator?"

Mo nodded. "Can you believe it? Nearly scared me half to death in the closet, let me tell you. I thought it was a piece of luggage."

Sam's mind raced. If it wasn't the alligator from the cage that they followed down into the passageway.... He shivered as a breeze blew through the bell tower.

Mo seemed to notice too. "I'm cold. Let's get you boys back to your parents." He pointed down to the trap door. "It's real late. They're going to be missing you right about now, I'll bet."

CHAPTER TWENTY

W hen they finally emerged from the bell tower, Mo opened the door on the top-floor stairwell with a key. It felt good to be back in the hotel. The long halls were eerily still and quiet at this late hour. Sam wanted to find Mom and Dad and tell them what had happened.

They reached the lobby from the main guest elevator just as Mom and Dad and Anita and Robert were coming in from the street.

"Boys?" Mom said when she saw them, her mouth opened wide. Sam knew they had some explaining to do. As usual. That seemed to happen a lot when he and Derek were trying to solve a mystery.

"Hey guys!" said Derek, with a devilish grin. "Is this the way to the late-night karaoke contest?"

Mom scrunched her eyebrows together, making an

all-too-recognizable crease across her forehead that usually meant they were about to get a lecture.

Robert and Anita walked up to Nathan with concerned looks. "What are you doing up this late?" said Robert, looking at his watch.

"Is the time change playing tricks on you?" asked Anita.

"No, dear, that would be the other way around—" said Robert.

"I took your rings," Nathan blurted out before Robert could finish his sentence.

There was nothing but silence for a moment. Anita blinked her eyes. "Excuse me?"

"What the devil are you talking about, Nathan?" Robert said, frowning.

"The wedding rings," Nathan answered quietly. "I'm the one who took them." He pulled the remaining ring out of his pocket and gave it to Anita.

"*You* took them?" said Robert, a puzzled look on his face.

"I don't understand, Nathan," said Anita. "Why would you take the rings?"

Nathan lowered his head and stared at his shoes, tears already streaming down his cheeks. "I don't know... I was trying to stop the wedding. I'm sorry."

"Where have you boys been?" Sam's dad said to the two of them.

Sam tried to think of a reasonable way to explain

what they'd been up to but nothing came to mind. Derek jumped in before he could say anything, starting his story again from the beginning. The adults were all too shocked to comment, so he just kept talking. He was on a roll, and there was no stopping him when he knew that he had an interested audience.

"We thought the alligators were chasing us," he finished, "so we climbed up into the bell tower—"

"The bell tower!" exclaimed Anita.

"But Mo came and saved us when we rang the bell," continued Derek. "And he helped Nathan off the ledge."

Mom and Dad and Robert and Anita just listened as Derek spoke, their wide eyes saying more than any words could. Dad rubbed his temples like he had a migraine. Sometimes he told people that he got all his gray hairs from what his boys put him through.

Sam just nodded his head and smiled sheepishly. Derek was always better at retelling their adventures than he was. Not that Mom and Dad usually believed everything. Even if it was true.

When Derek was finally quiet, Robert looked at Nathan like he was about to say something harsh. Before he could speak, Anita stepped forward and draped her arms around Nathan's shoulders. "I'm sorry that you're not happy about the wedding, Nathan. I know that it has to be hard for you."

Nathan just nodded his head, wiping away tears.

"But listen," Anita continued, "we will all take this slow. I'll give you as much room as you need." Sam noticed for the first time what a caring face she had. It made sense to him that she was Mom's close friend.

Nathan looked up at Robert, who nodded back. "You are a very important part of this family." He pulled Nathan's chin up with his hand and looked into his eyes. "Okay?"

"Okay." Nathan wiped his eyes and nodded. "I'm sorry."

Robert put one arm around Nathan, the other around Anita. He looked up at Mom and Dad. "This family business isn't easy, is it?"

Mom looked at Sam and Derek and smiled. "No."

"But it's the best business you can be in," said Dad.

"Just think," said Derek, gesturing at himself and Sam. "At least you don't have to deal with us."

Everyone laughed.

Just then, Mo and the hotel manager walked up to the group from the parking lot. "I trust everything is all right, Mr. Wanderfelt?"

Robert nodded. "We're just great, thank you."

Mo stepped over to Nathan, holding something in his hand. "Look what I found."

Nathan's face brightened. "The ring!"

"Hey!" shouted Sam. "You found it."

"All part of the job," said Mo, grinning.

Sam felt bad for ever suspecting Mo of being the thief. He was such a nice guy. He supposed he had let the mystery get the best of him.

"Did you know they found the alligator, Mom?" said Derek, pointing into the Rotunda.

"One of them, at least," said Sam.

"We heard!" replied Dad. "The hotel manager came over and told us across the street."

"Such a relief!" exclaimed Mr. Wonderful.

"Well I'm glad things are working out," said Mom. "But it is very late."

"That's right," said Anita. "I think we all need to get some sleep."

"We have a wedding tomorrow!" said Robert, squeezing Anita tight.

Sam yawned. He realized how tired he was and nodded. He'd almost forgotten about the wedding.

* * *

DAD SAID they were going to talk about their late night exploring more when they got home. In the meantime, he told the boys not to worry and go to sleep. Easy for him to say. He hadn't seen the lake of alligators.

Even if none of the grownups believed them, Sam still couldn't get that image out of his mind. What if they wandered back up into the hotel? He was a notoriously sound sleeper. He might not even hear an alligator attack!

He got up and walked to the bathroom for a drink of water. Before he did, he slowly glanced behind the shower curtain just to make sure nothing was lurking.

"What are you doing?" whispered Derek, as Sam tiptoed back into the room.

He lay back down in his bed. "Can't sleep."

"Yeah, me neither."

"I just—" Sam hesitated, not sure if he wanted to open himself up to teasing from his brother. "I keep thinking about things."

"Alligators?"

"Yeah."

"Me, too," said Derek, turning over to see the clock on his nightstand.

"You do?"

"Sure," said Derek. "I can't decide if it was the caged alligator I saw disappear by the stairs, or if it was one of the wild ones. Maybe they come up here all the time. I mean, it's freaky to think about all those alligators living in the tunnels under the hotel. How long have they been there? How many are there? Do they really creep up into the building when it's cold? Are they trapped in Alligator Lake now, since the rocks fell in front of the doorway when we ran?"

Sam just nodded. He was relieved to hear that he wasn't alone. Surprised, but relieved.

He lay back down and closed his eyes. He tried to clear his mind. He didn't want to think about alligators anymore. "Goodnight."

"Goodnight."

Eventually he must have faded off to sleep. The last thing he remembered thinking about was dozens of alligators sledding down the grand staircase. They didn't even need sleds, they just slid along on their bellies, all the way across the Rotunda.

———

CHAPTER TWENTY-ONE

I t was time for the big event. The guests were filing into the Rotunda Lobby for the wedding. Sam and Derek stood on opposite sides of the back entrance handing out programs.

"I still think we should try to charge for these," said Derek, smiling.

"Maybe Mr. Wonderful will pay us afterward for doing a good job," said Sam.

He looked across the room. Gold-colored chairs were lined up in rows. Ushers dressed in tuxedoes walked the female guests to their seats, the men following behind. Instead of walking down the aisle from the back like most weddings, the processional would come down the grand staircase toward everyone, with the ceremony at the bottom of the stairs.

Sam had to admit, it was pretty nice. He could see why Anita and Robert chose The Jefferson for the wedding ceremony. If only he didn't have to wear his tie. Sam tugged on it gently, hoping to get a little more breathing room underneath his top button.

"Looking good, boys," said Dad, walking toward them.

Sam handed him a program. "Thanks."

"It's not too hard for me," said Derek, "but Sam's made a big effort."

"Are you keeping an eye on your friend?" asked Dad, gesturing across the room.

Sam pretended to laugh. "I guess." He looked over at the alligator cage, set up next to them in the back of the Rotunda on a pedestal. Red velvet ropes were stationed all around to keep anyone from getting too close. A heavy padlock secured the latch on the door. The hotel manager had positioned Mo near the cage, standing guard just in case anyone didn't get the message. At least by now they had learned their lesson. Sam just wished it had been a little sooner.

"I don't think he's going anywhere," said Derek. He looked over at Dad. "Unless you want me to try to make things a little more interesting…"

Dad gave him a stern frown before walking into the Rotunda. "Don't get any ideas. I'll hold two seats for you in my row. Come sit down once the guests have finished coming in."

"Okay," said Sam, flipping through his pile of programs.

A woman playing soft music on a grand piano next

to the staircase changed tunes into something more formal. Caitlin's dad moved into position at the front of the room with his camera. He had another assistant at the top of the stairs who would capture the photos of the wedding party coming down.

Caitlin followed her dad, holding an extra camera and a large flash. She looked pretty in a light pink dress. Sam was impressed, she really seemed to know what she was doing. Maybe she was right after all. In that elegant room, surrounded by history and decorations, it did feel like a movie.

After the last guest entered the Rotunda, Sam and Derek joined their dad in the second row. Robert and three groomsmen stepped out from the side of the room and lined up at the bottom of the grand staircase. They were all dressed in black tuxedos, just like the ushers. Sam smiled as he saw Nathan standing next to his dad in his tux as the best man. He was short, but he looked good.

The piano tune changed to a stately processional that Sam recognized, but he didn't know the name of. Two bridesmaids came first, slowly stepping down the grand staircase. Each wore a long yellow dress and held a simple bouquet of white roses.

Sam felt chill bumps on his arms, like a cool breeze. His attention shifted to the side of the staircase. What was that? Something had moved, he was sure of it. He glanced around, but no one else had noticed. They were all concentrating on the wedding party coming down the stairs. He turned to look at Mo standing guard in the back of the room. The alligator was still in its cage. Thank goodness. Sam took a deep breath. Why was he so jumpy?

Derek nudged Sam with his elbow, nodding to the top of the stairs. Mom was coming down. She looked pretty in her yellow dress. Her hair was pulled up in a way that he'd never seen. She looked down at them and winked.

He took his eyes off Mo and stretched his neck to look beside the staircase. A dark shadow filled the floor right in front of the spot in the wall where they'd entered the passageway. Sam gulped. Something moved. Was that a leg? He poked Derek.

"Stop!" Derek whispered, pushing Sam's hand away. Anita was at the crest of the staircase. Her long white gown trailed several feet behind her, stretching out on the red carpet of the staircase. Sam's eyes darted back and forth from the side of the staircase to the red carpet. He glimpsed Anita's white alligator shoes when she lifted the edge of her gown to walk.

When he looked back at the spot next to the stairs, the shadow was gone. He blinked his eyes. Had something been there or was his imagination just getting the best of him?

Anita reached the bottom step, and Robert moved over to meet her. Sam looked up at Dad and saw his face in a smile, his eyes still fixed on Mom. Should he say something? As Robert and Anita held hands and the minister started speaking, Sam sighed and shook his head. He needed to get alligators out of his mind.

* * *

"LADIES AND GENTLEMEN," the band leader's voice said over the loudspeaker, "we're going to slow this one down a bit."

Sam took a long sip of his punch as the band started playing a romantic tune. The wedding reception was in a large ballroom off the Rotunda.

"Aren't you going to ask me to dance, Sam Jackson?"

Sam looked up at Caitlin standing in front of him. Where had she come from? He gave a nervous smile. "Uh…"

"Of course he will, Caitlin," his mom answered, nudging him toward the dance floor.

Sam felt his stomach tighten. His cheeks burned. He looked up at his mom with pleading eyes, but she just smiled.

Caitlin set her camera down on the table and walked with him onto the dance floor. Before he knew it, her hands were resting on his shoulders. He looked at the couple next to him and awkwardly copied how the man had his hands on the woman's waist. He began shuffling his feet back and forth, following the flow of the music. Sort of.

Sam looked up at Caitlin. She was smiling, staring around the room. He tried to breathe. This wasn't so bad.

"Ouch!" Caitlin said, moving her foot back. He'd stepped on her toe.

"Sorry," he muttered, trying not to sweat. "I don't really know how to dance."

Caitlin giggled. "Me either." She glanced around them. "But I think we're doing okay. No one seems to be staring."

They turned and saw Derek on the side of the room making funny faces at them.

"Much," she added.

Sam laughed. He started to relax. That was one of the reasons he liked being friends with Caitlin. She was easy to be around.

"Do you think they're going to be happy?" Caitlin asked, nodding at Robert and Anita on the other side of the dance floor.

"I guess," said Sam. "They seem to be happy now, right?"

Caitlin nodded. "I hope so."

Sam looked at Nathan, sitting on the side of the room. "What about him?"

"I think he's coming around," said Caitlin. "I'm sure it will be hard though, with all the changes in his life. My mom says that everyone handles changes differently."

"Yeah," nodded Sam. He was starting to get the hang of this dancing stuff.

"There's just one thing I don't get," said Caitlin.

"What?"

"Who let the alligator out of the cage?"

Sam shrugged. He'd been thinking about that too. "Maybe it just escaped."

"By itself?" asked Caitlin.

"Maybe it was homesick." He thought of the under-ground lake and all the alligators gathered around it. "Maybe the zoo alligator could sense all the others in the passageway. Maybe he was just trying to go home." He nodded over at Nathan. "It's hard to be in a new place sometimes."

The slow song ended and Caitlin pulled her arms tighter around Sam's neck and hugged him. "Thanks for the dance."

Sam nodded and stepped back as a new song started up. Derek rushed over to them with a big grin. Sam put his hand up. "Don't say a word."

"What?" laughed Derek, dancing to the new song. It was faster than the last one. He looked over at Caitlin. "How do you like my moves?"

Nathan walked up to their group. He snickered at Derek. "Is that supposed to be dancing?"

"You know it," answered Derek.

"Hey, I love this song!" said Caitlin, recognizing the tune. "It's perfect, don't you think?"

"What is it?" asked Sam.

Nathan looked surprised. "You don't know Elton John? He's from England. It's brilliant!"

Sam listened to the words and started laughing.

"La, la, la, la, la, la!" sang Derek, rocking along to the mad piano playing. "This is *Crocodile Rock*!"

CHAPTER TWENTY-TWO

S am was happy to finally be going home. It felt good to know that he'd be sleeping in his own bed without any fear of reptiles gobbling him up while he slept. He thought about all the crazy things that had happened that weekend at The Jefferson. He never imagined that a wedding could be so stressful, especially for a guest!

After the ceremony, he and Derek had led Mo and the hotel manager down through the secret passageway under the grand staircase. Things looked much different all lit up by flashlights. They felt different too with shoes on Sam's feet and regular clothes instead of pajamas.

They found the old room with Lewis Ginter's name on it. The men both marveled about the world map on the wall with Ginter's travel markings, and some of the other documents in the desk and shelves were quite rare. The manager said the discovered items would make great additions to the display cases up in the hotel.

Derek tried to lead the way back to Alligator Lake, but it was hard to remember where they'd been. The twists and turns in the passageways were confusing. Mo was worried that they might get lost and the hotel manager acted nervous being in the tunnels. Both grownups seemed skeptical that the boys had really seen a lake of alligators underground.

They had finally found what looked like the doorway they'd entered on the way to the room with the alligators, but now it was just a tall pile of crumbled rocks. Sam remembered slamming into the beams and the avalanche of rocks as they ran away. It did seem like the same spot, but he couldn't be sure if the rock pile had just formed the night before or had been there for decades.

There was no trace of a fire in the tunnels, much to the relief of the hotel manager. He said that one hotel fire in 1901 was enough. Nor were there any signs of alligators. Not that Sam wanted to find any. After a while, he had even started wondering if they'd dreamed the whole thing up, but deep down he knew they hadn't. Besides, Derek and Nathan had seen it too.

Alligator Lake was real, even if it was buried behind a pile of rocks. Sam could still see the alligator's beady eyes staring at him through the lantern light. He could feel the heat from the fire against his face. He shuddered again just thinking about it.

When they pulled into the driveway, Mr. Haskins

waved at them from over his fence. Sam remembered what they'd said to him before the wedding, when he showed them the old picture from his wallet. They'd promised to tell him if anything crazy with alligators had happened. Well that was an understatement.

Derek told the old man about meeting Mo and everything they'd seen in the passageways. Mr. Haskins just listened, taking it all in with his usual crooked smile. Sam didn't know if he believed their story either, but there was a glimmer in his eyes that said he just might.

There was something about that old hotel that seemed like it would stick in one's memory. Maybe it was all the history, the long staircase, or just the alligators. Whatever it was, Sam knew he wouldn't forget it either.

Perhaps someday he'd be an old man like Mr. Haskins, and he'd tell some kids all about the crazy scary weekend that he went to The Jefferson for a wedding, and along the way, met its most unusual guests.

MIDNIGHT AT THE MANSION

THE VIRGINIA MYSTERIES BOOK 5

Sam, Derek, and Caitlin have encountered many mysteries together, but when they visit Maymont, Richmond's historic estate, danger is lurking at every turn. A chance meeting with a mysterious stranger leads to a frantic chase and a desperate message to save Maymont's bald eagles. When Sam receives an eerie warning in the middle of the night, Derek and Caitlin devise a plan that leads them high into the Blue Ridge Mountains. To save the eagles, the kids must find a secret abandoned palace, survive the wilds of the Appalachian Trail and avoid capture by criminals, all before midnight.

ACKNOWLEDGMENTS

Visiting historical places like The Jefferson is one of my favorite things. It's a mandatory visit if you are in downtown Richmond and have the time. A picture of the staircase and the Rotunda always gets one of the biggest ooh's and ahh's from from students during my many school visits. It's hard not to let your imagination run wild in such a gorgeous place, alligators or not. Thanks to Pat Smith for so generously featuring my books in the Gator Gifts shop. Lewis Ginter is a fascinating person to learn about, with The Jefferson being just one of his many endeavors and accomplishments.

If I'd tried to peer up ahead three years ago, I wouldn't have suspected where this road would lead. Thousands of books sold, hundreds of kids and families that I've been able to meet. As Sam would say, it's been sweet!

The generous supply of grace from my family means

so much. I couldn't do this without their inspiration and patience. Thank you to my wife, Mary, and my three boys, Matthew, Josh, and Aaron, for cheering me on along the journey and allowing me to stretch for my passions.

Thank you also to so many friends and family who have supported my efforts and provided enthusiasm and encouragement - Alicia, Ryan, Mom, Dad, Jean, Ray Robin, Julia, Richmond Children's Writers critique group, CHAT, Ali, and Julie. Thanks to my editor, Kim Sheard at Another View Editing for keeping everything clear and concise, Janie Dullard at Lector's Books for her proofreading, and Dane at Ebook Launch for designing all the awesome covers for the series.

To Virginia, my adopted home, thank you for bursting with history, and for the enthusiasm of all who live here for learning about and from its past.

ABOUT THE AUTHOR

Steven K. Smith is the author of *The Virginia Mysteries*, *Brother Wars*, and *Final Kingdom* series for middle grade readers. He lives with his wife, three young sons, and a golden retriever in Richmond, Virginia.

For more information, visit:

www.stevenksmith.net

steve@myboys3.com

ALSO BY STEVEN K. SMITH

THE VIRGINIA MYSTERIES:

Summer of the Woods

Mystery on Church Hill

Ghosts of Belle Isle

Secret of the Staircase

Midnight at the Mansion

Shadows at Jamestown

Spies at Mount Vernon

Escape from Monticello

BROTHER WARS SERIES:

Brother Wars

Cabin Eleven

The Big Apple

FINAL KINGDOM TRILOGY (10+):

The Missing

The Recruit

The Bridge

MYBOYS3 PRESS SUPPORTS

CHAT

Sam, Derek, and Caitlin aren't the only kids who crave adventure. Whether near woods in the country or amidst tall buildings and the busy urban streets of a city, every child needs exciting ways to explore his or her imagination, excel at learning and have fun.

A portion of the proceeds from *The Virginia Mysteries* series will be donated to the great work of **CHAT (Church Hill Activities & Tutoring)**. CHAT is a non-profit group that works with kids in the Church Hill neighborhood of inner-city Richmond, Virginia.

To learn more about CHAT, including opportunities to volunteer or contribute financially, visit **www. chatrichmond.org**.

DID YOU ENJOY SECRET OF THE STAIRCASE?

WOULD YOU ... REVIEW?

Online reviews are crucial for indie authors like me. They help bring credibility and make books more discoverable by new readers. No matter where you purchased your book, if you could take a few moments and give an honest review at one of the following websites, I'd be so grateful.

Amazon.com
Goodreads.com

Thank you and thanks for reading!

Steve